Khunda

Khunda

Ancient Blood Book One

ISBN: 978-1-7332747-0-8 (paperback)
ISBN: 978-1-7332747-1-5 (ebook)

To Dustin,

Thank you for being my other half.

Chapter One

Lexy Greggs, Captain of the Khunda, pressed her dark hair deeper into the headrest as she stole a quick look at Z, her pilot and best friend. He lowered the large ship into the dark shadows of an asteroid in the dead zone of the Corvus constellation and then squeezed his eyes closed. The air inside the bridge was thick; after all, they were running from a ship full of pissed off mercenaries.

This wasn't their first time in this position. Lexy took a deep breath as her mind drifted back to the events of the past few years. The Royal planets had become more dangerous as rumors of a rebellion in the outer planets spread. Ameran, the Director of the Capital Transport Agency or CTA as everyone called it, was having a hard time hiring and keeping security officers. That's how they ended up on a mission with passengers and no security.

Silently, they watched as the mercenary ship passed them, unaware the Khunda was hiding less than a mile away. Just then the metal of the ship's outer hull moaned and Lexy's heart leapt in her chest. She drew in a sharp breath, but the ship passed by with no indication of seeing them. Even so, Lexy held up her hand to maintain silence on the bridge. Seconds dragged on. Finally, she released the air trapped in her lungs and dropped her hand.

"I think we're good. Can you get us out of the dead zone? " Lexy asked.

Z released his grip on the armrests, "Yes, ma'am." he replied.

Z and Lexy had been best friends since they were kids, even though sometimes they were separated by galaxies. Z was a gray alien standing four feet tall. He wore the CTA's steel blue jumpsuit with a set of wings on his collar and a pair of black boots. Lexy wore the same uniform, except she had two Captains Stars on her collar.

Z eased the ship back into open space, "That was close," he said.

"I know. Don't ever do that to me again," Lexy teased.

"I wasn't the one who had to insult his mother. There are things you don't do, and that is one of them." Z said, bringing the flight plans up on his console and typing in their destination.

Lexy shook her head, "He's a grown man, and if he couldn't take it he shouldn't have started it." Lexy tapped a button labeled all speakers. "Sorry about the bumpy ride folks, we're back on course to the Leo Constellation."

"Beep. Beep. Beep," the console sounded as a red light began flashing.

"Lexy! You might want to nix that last message, 'cause they're baa-ack," Z said, buckling his restraints.

"Shit!" Punching the button again, Lexy yelled, "Never mind, I take it back. Sit down and buckle up!"

Z pushed the engines into gear and the Khunda gave a jolt of protest.

Lexy pointed at the window, "Don't forget we still have-"

"Yes, yes, I see the big rocks!" Z said, maneuvering the ship with ease past several pieces of a nearby fragmented planet. He rolled his eyes as Lexy cringed with every close encounter while simultaneously pressing her feet into the console and pushing her back against the chair as those to brace herself from some imagined impact.

"Go left...watch it…you're a bit...oh geez!...Right. Right. Right...Go.Go. GO!" she yelled.

"You are the worst side seat, driver. Don't make me kick you out," Z snapped, his face pinched in concentration.

They wove through the debris and were almost home free when blue lights flew past them.

"What was that?" Lexy asked, sitting up. "Did they shoot at us?"

"I think they did," Z said, as two more lights flashed past them, "Yep, I'd say they are shooting at us."

Lexy sat back, anger replacing the fear on her face, "No one shoots at Khunda; it's my ship! Open up a com to that scumbag."

The automated but pleasant voice responded, "Yes, captain ... Coms linked."

The mercenaries' laughter filled the control room.

"Are you shitting me?" Lexy asked, looking at Z. "For your information, you bastards shot at the Khunda, a Royal Class A transport ship and I am now, by royal law, allowed to fire back. Either give up your pursuit or suffer the consequences."

The mercenaries laughed louder than before.

"The Khunda? So I presume I am speaking to Captain Greggs, Ameran's favorite Earthling Captain. Don't worry, I will kill you long before I rip apart your ship and sell it for parts. As for your passengers, I hear they have some tech that would fetch a nice price from the right buyer. Not that you'll be alive to find out."

The raspy voice was that of Captain Adohan, once a decorated war Captain, now a hired gun and top five on the royal wanted list. He owned one of the few mercenary ships ballsy enough to torment the enlightened planets. How such a celebrated hero could turn into a vicious pirate was beyond Lexy. His threats made her blood boil.

"You asked for it, pig! Khunda out!" she said, unfastening her restraints and jumping out of her chair. "Khunda, shields at max and give me full control of weapons."

The ship jerked and Lexy stumbled; the auto-gravity must have been damaged when they clipped a cliff trying to hide. She threw herself into one of the two weapons chairs against the back wall and once strapped in, she leaned back. A HoloScreen appeared in front of her eyes, giving her a full 360 degree view around them. They were surrounded by darkness and floating debris. The dead zone had once been a flourishing planet system, but hundreds of years ago a war broke out and the main planet and all of the beings living on it were destroyed. In the aftermath, the Royal system was created.

"Khunda, full charge of all weapons," Lexy said.

"Yes, captain," Khunda responded.

The female's voice was calm, while Lexy's heart felt like it was going to pound out of her chest. She felt her thoughts connecting to the ship's weapons system. As a half biological and half technological ship, Khunda was able to interpret neural impulses through a band Lexy wore on her wrist.

Lexy looked around for Adohan's ship. It was a war grade cargo carrier. The hull was tall, with two cargo doors allowing for faster loading. The ship's exterior was scared with laser burns. From this distance Lexy could make out the spot where the Royal Guard symbol used to be. Adohan must have painted over it when he defected to the other side. Lining up her sights, Lexy fired at the ship, missing by a hair. She aimed again, this time grazing their side.

"Yes, sucker. Bring it on," she yelled.

They returned fire. Z lurched the Khunda just in time. "Hey, Lex how about a little less trash talk and a little more shooting!" he said.

"Oh, you're just mad 'cause I get to play with our new friends," she joked.

She had the ship in her sights and was about to fire again when the Khunda jolted to the left.

"Oops, clipped a wing," Z said, shrugging.

He pulled back on the power to the engines. Lexy looked for her target, eyes scanning across the black space, but she couldn't find the mercenary ship. She flipped the switch to infrared.

"Um, Z-" she started.

The Khunda slammed to a stop.

"Found 'em," Z said in a stiff voice.

Lexy sat up, disconnecting herself from the

weapons and followed Z's gaze. The ship was in front of them, weapons armed and waiting. She knew Adohan was hoping she would surrender in an effort to save the lives of her cargo. He wouldn't hesitate to blow them to pieces before Khunda's laser pulse based weapons could build enough power to fire. The only hope they had was to try and escape.

Lexy threw herself into the Captain's chair and quickly strapped in while her mind raced to find a solution that didn't end in getting shot. Crap! How did we end up in this situation?

Z tilted his head toward Lexy, but his eyes remained on the screen.

"Got any ideas?" he asked.

Her eyes remaining locked on Adohan's ship for a moment, but when they flicked over to meet Z's she said the only thing that came to mind, "Wanna try a flip-cover?"

Z's large black eyes widened in shock, "I thought we agreed to never try that again?"

"Um, I don't think we have a choice," she stated.

"Fine, but if I burn out the thrusters again you get to explain it to the Director."

"Sure, as long as you explain the chip out of our side," she said flatly.

"I was trying to dodge a-," Z sighed, "Deal."

Z and Director Ameran didn't always see eye to

eye. Ameran thought Z needed to be more respectful to his superiors, while Z thought she needed to get laid. Lexy constantly found herself trying to smooth things over between them.

"On three," Lexy said, pressing icons on the console. She could see Z gripping the throttle. "One. Two. Three!"

Z jerked the control all the way back, slamming both him and Lexy forward against their restraints. As the Khunda sped backward, Adohan's ship followed and was beginning to close in on them. Z grabbed the steering control with his left hand and took a deep breath.

"This is gonna hurt."

Jamming the gear control all the way forward, he pulled the steering as far toward him as he could. The ship did a backflip to face the opposite direction. Hanging upside down in their restraints, Lexy pulled the lever and the Khunda released a large parachute-like fabric from its' back end. As they hoped, the fabric covered Adohan's ship. Lexy pulled the lever back another notch, releasing the fabric. Z turned the steering, flipping the Khunda upright. Breathing heavily, they started laughing.

"Holy shit! It worked," Lexy said, "Now get us the hell out of here."

Still laughing, Z pushed the engines and the Khunda disappeared into the darkness.

A week later Lexy was safe, back at home on Earth. She had lived in Montana for most of her life with her parents who worked for the CTA. It was rare to hire Earthlings at that time, but her mother was half Royal and best friends with Ameran, whose father was the Director of the CTA. Z's father worked on her parent's ship and they were all friends. Which is how she and Z became best friends. When Lexy was sixteen her aunt May and uncle Greggs took her in after her parent's ship was attacked by mercenaries, and they were killed while protecting their cargo. Her aunt and uncle already knew about the existence of aliens. They were known as Enlightened Earthlings and came from long lineages of families who helped cover up their existence.

Aunt May told Lexy that she needed a degree from Earth as well as her training to be a Captain in space. So, Lexy got her bachelor's degree in creative writing after she got her Captain's rank at the Royal Intergalactic Academy, which she attended with Z. Everyone went through two years as members of the Royal Guard after the academy and when she wasn't stationed on some corner of the galaxy she would be on Earth taking classes like any normal person. Her stories of a space captain and her pilot always thrilled her professors, so, after college, Lexy began to publish the misadventures that she and Z had. The books soon became bestsellers.

After her first three books, Lexy bought a couple of acres and built the two-bedroom cottage. She planned to build onto it if there was ever a need to, but for now, it was the perfect size for her and Bones, her black German Shepard and other best friend.

Lexy was sitting with her toes tucked under Bones who was taking up the other half of the couch. She was answering email from her publisher and enjoying the stillness that can only be found in nature. Her sliding back door was open allowing the cool fall air to circulate through the cottage.

A chirp came from her CTA issued tablet sitting on the coffee table. She leaned over, picked it up and pressed the bubble that appeared on the screen. It was a message from her CTA doctor clearing her for regular duty. After the last mission she had a couple of bumps and bruises but everyone got home safe.

She set the tablet back on the table and wiggled her toes to get Bones' attention, "I think it's time to go to bed, buddy," She said, smiling at his drowsy eyes.

"We have to help May with the farmer's market tomorrow and I have to start my new book," She explained, sliding her toes out from under the mound of fur, "I told May we would help her with the deliveries while I'm back as well so we have an early morning."

Bones stretched his paws and slid off the couch. Lexy cleaned her cup in the sink while Bones took himself outside to use the bathroom. When he was done, she closed the door and got ready for bed. Bones cuddled next to her legs when she got into bed.

She enjoyed the calm moments on Earth, especially after a rough transport in space. She hoped their next job wouldn't bring any surprises.

Chapter Two

Trent pulled the sheet higher on his shoulder. The air had grown colder overnight. He was still adjusting to the September weather in Montana. It was five in the morning and his warm bed was holding him hostage, but every time he closed his eyes, the unpacked boxes and running to-do list kept him from going back to sleep.

He flopped onto his back, kicking off the covers and stretching to wake up the rest of his limbs. After spending a decade in the Army, his internal alarm clock woke him up before the sun decided to make an appearance. He didn't need to be at work until five that night, so he had enough time to unpack a box of warm clothes, grab some coffee and do a grocery run. He'd had about all he could take of fried foods and was in desperate need of a home-cooked meal. For the last couple of weeks, he'd eaten at every restaurant, bar, and diner he could find since his new apartment was within walking distance to the downtown area, which made the choice to eat out that much easier. But he knew he had to start saving money for when the bills began to roll in, so no more eating out.

Trent finally rolled out of bed and navigated to the closet, grabbing a dark gray sweater from one of the boxes scattered all over the floor. When he pulled it down over his head his eyes fell on the Amazon boxes stashed in the corner; the stuff his mother was sending was adding to the mess. He cringed at the amount of unpacking he still had to do and then began to get a jump on it by pulling his winter clothes out of a box. When they were all hung up or put in the dresser he made a mental note to shop for clothes that would survive the winters up here. His current wardrobe was perfect for the much warmer weather in Georgia, his home state, although he did own some snowboarding gear.

After brushing his teeth, splashing some water on his face and running a comb through his hair, Trent tucked his wallet into a back pocket and left the apartment building on foot. He liked the walk into town. The fresh air cleared his mind. Central Avenue had shopping, dining, and stunning mountain views. As he walked down the main drag heading to his favorite coffee shop he remembered the exact moment he decided to move to Whitefish. A group of his buddies had planned a snowboarding trip up here and after spending a week of days on the slopes followed by nights on the town he couldn't see himself anywhere else.

Trent's muscles relaxed as he walked into the Red Caboose and the smell of freshly brewed coffee welcomed him. A few people were scattered around the diner, sitting at wooden tables with their hands wrapped snugly around steaming cups. He stepped up to the counter where a familiar blonde smiled at him. Her name was Sally, but that was about all he knew other than she ran the register most mornings.

"Hi, Trent. Would you like your usual?"

He smiled; it was good to have a usual.

"Yes, please," he replied.

She punched in his order and swiped the card he handed her, "Are you working tonight?"

"Yeah, my first overnight shift."

"Oh, too bad. A group of us were going to hang out at the Red Room tonight."

Trent knew she was fishing for a date. She had been since they met on his first day in town.

"Maybe next time," he said.

Smiling at her, he picked up his coffee and walked to the door, but as he reached for the handle it swung open, nearly hitting him. A woman chatting animatedly on her cell phone mumbled an apology as she brushed past him. He shook his head as he stared after her. She wore jeans, a leather jacket, and her hair was tucked under a baseball cap.

She looked to be around her late twenties. She must live here because Sally asked her if she wanted her usual too.

Trent stepped outside, freezing when he saw a large black German Shepherd sitting on the sidewalk, his leash curled on the ground next to him. The dog stared at Trent.

Trent stared back, unsure of the dog's intentions.

"Bones!" an older lady said, walking up to the dog and throwing her arms around him. The dog licked her face, as his tail spun in happy circles.

That's odd?

Trent walked away when the lady started asking the dog questions and acting like he was responding to them.

The rest of Trent's morning was spent unpacking the groceries he bought on his way home. Then his mother called and talked for an hour about neighborhood gossip. He let her go on about how the Schmits' son was divorcing his second wife and that Sarah from three houses down was pregnant again. His mother was always well informed of the goings-on. She worked part-time with the local PAL (Police Athletic League) program. Having grown up attending pub-lic safety events, Trent knew he wanted to be in law en-forcement. After hanging up with his mom, he decided it would be a good idea to take a nap before his first overnight shift. So, he slid under his comforter and allowed himself to fall asleep.

The department was quiet, as it normally was. The good thing about working in a tourist town was that not much happened beyond the occasional bar fight or wild animal sightings. Trent waved at the receptionist, Mrs. Wilson, as he walked into the police department for roll call. She gave him a quick wave in return and continued reading her trashy magazine. Chief Greggs was in the roll call room when Trent walked in.

"Trent, first night shift?" Greggs asked.

"Yes, sir," Trent replied.

Greggs' large figure flipped through a stack of files. Trent could see how Greggs used his size to intimidate lawbreakers.

"Want a tip? Stay away from Bookworks from seven to nine. They have a monthly book club that meets there and this month they're reading a romance novel," Greggs warned.

He looked at Trent over the top of his glasses. "Mrs. Greggs said she read it last year and found it … inspiring," Greggs said with a chuckle, bouncing his eyebrows up and down.

Trent cringed at the thought, "Thanks for the warning," he said.

"Do you mind patrolling the farmer's market

tonight? There will be a lot of people there and you never know what could happen. I have everyone spread out across town. It's that time of year when the bears get closer to town searching for food."

"Sure thing," Trent replied.

Trent left the department and parked his patrol car on Central Avenue. He started his patrol through the market in Depot Park. Locals and tourists hurried from table to table buying goods and chatting about local gossip. Trent checked his watch. It was 5:45 and the market was just getting started. He walked around the edge of the park, scaring off a couple of teenagers that were openly "getting to know each other".

"Sorry," the boy shrugged.

The girl winked at Trent as they rushed away.

Trent smiled, remembering when he was a teen.

A black blur flew past him. He recognized that spinning tail.

"Hey!" Trent followed the dog, whistling and calling out to him. "Come here, boy."

The dog slid to a stop next to a picnic table and sat down. A woman, typing on her laptop, reached down without taking her eyes off the screen and scratched the dog's head.

"Uh, miss, is that your dog?" Trent asked.

The woman looked at him, "Are you the new officer?"

"Uh, yes." *Smooth dude.*

"This is Bones," she nodded to the dog, "if you have any more questions about him, you can ask Chief Greggs."

Trent slid his thumbs under his duty belt, "You know the Chief?"

The woman sighed, tossing her bag onto the table.

"Bones is harmless. Although I can see how a newbie like yourself could be scared," she said, pulling a baseball cap out of her bag and then shoving in her laptop.

Trent recognized the cap.

"You were at the coffee shop today. You almost ran me over."

The woman shrugged, "I apologized."

Trent stepped forward to reply, but stopped when Bones stood, his ears perked at full attention.

He threw his hands up, smiling, in surrender, "You really should have him on a leash."

A large hand slapped him on the back.

From behind him Greggs said, "Bones wouldn't hurt a fly unless that fly threatened his mama," he said.

Chief Greggs passed Trent, walked to the woman and kissed her on the head.

"You must be the Chief's niece then," Trent said.

He remembered the first time he met the Chief's wife, May, she went on and on about how their niece was a SciFi writer.

Trent looked at Bones, "Can I introduce myself to your owner?"

Bones sat, his tail wagging.

Trent walked up to girl, extended his hand and said, "My name is Trent. It's nice to finally meet you."

The woman looked at his hand; Greggs pushed his shoulder into hers.

"Hi, I'm Lexy."

They shook hands.

Greggs cleared his throat, "Lex, May was looking for some help. How about you show Trent where he can buy the best pies in Whitefish."

"But I have-" Lexy began.

Greggs gave her a stern look.

"This way Officer," Lexy slung her bag over her shoulder and headed toward the market.

Greggs smiled, "We are still trying to work on her social skills."

Bones walked up to Trent, his tail wagging in happy circles again. Trent reached down and scratched his head, "It's nice to meet you too, boy."

Lexy yelled over her shoulder, "May won't wait

forever."

Bones huffed and followed Lexy as she wove her way through the mass of shoppers.

"What have I gotten myself into?" Trent mumbled.

May was a stout older lady with a maternal face. Greggs was right, her pies were the best. As soon as Trent arrived at her stand a piece of apple pie magically appeared in his hand. He watched her sell pies as if everyone was family. She knew their names, their kid's names and asked how ill loved ones were doing.

Lexy began helping by packing orders and taking money as soon as she got to the stand. Every once in a while she glanced at Trent, who spent his time chatting with locals as they asked if he was new in town, where he was from, and what his relationship status was. He was happy to answer their questions and listen to their stories. A part of being a small town officer was getting to know the community, and Trent was doing his best to fit in.

"You really should make a sign and hang it from your neck, 'Yes, I'm new here'," Lexy said.

Trent chuckled, "I don't think it'll match my uniform."

"I can talk to my uncle for you if you want."

Lexy handed him another piece of the pie. This time it was chocolate.

"I don't know if I can eat this. I'm still full from the five pieces your aunt gave me," Trent said.

Lexy narrowed her eyes at him, "Just so you know, I help make the chocolate pies. So, I may take offense if you refuse to eat it."

She handed him a plastic fork. Trent took it and dug into the pie.

"The only way she helps with the pies is by sampling the chocolate," May said as she arranged the pies on the table.

Lexy gave May a fake shocked look before saying, "As we all know, that is the most important part. If the chocolate tastes bad, what is the point of making a chocolate pie?"

"Yes, you're right, Lex." May rolled her eyes and turned to help a customer.

Lexy broke off a piece of crust and handed it to Bones, who had been waiting patiently next to the table.

"Besides, she banned me from using the oven, stand mixer and her kitchen in general when I was ten."

May spoke over her shoulder. "With good reason, as you will recall."

Lexy made a face, broke off another piece of crust and tossed it to Bones.

"And stop feeding Bones my pies. He has his own treats in my bag," May snapped.

As if he understood, Bones turned to May's purse and began smelling every inch of it.

Lexy grabbed the bag, found the treats and began handing them to Bones one-by-one.

"So, how was I for a host?" she asked Trent.

He tossed the plate into the trash. "Fine I guess. I didn't know I had to grade you."

"You don't, but if you feel like telling my uncle that I was nice to you, I would appreciate it."

"He did say something about socializing you. What's that about?"

Lexy rolled her eyes. "I guess May has told you I'm a writer?"

Trent nodded.

"Well, they seem to think I spend too much time working and not enough time doing what 'normal' people do."

Trent was beginning to understand, "Oh, I'm a pawn in their plan to make you normal."

"Basically," Lexy said.

She'd fed Bones the whole bag of treats and now he was sniffing her empty hands. Bones huffed at the lack of crumbs and sat back down next to the table.

"You know, shepherds are a smart breed. We used them in the military," Trent said, smiling at Bones.

"I think mine is broken because all he does is eat

and give me attitude," Lexy joked.

Bones cocked his head at Lexy.

"Don't worry, I still love you."

Trent was starting to see why Greggs thought she could use some human interaction. She began rearranging business cards on the table.

"Have you lived here your whole life?"

"Pretty much." Lexy shifted back on her heels. "You don't have to babysit, you know. I'm sure there's a crime that needs to be stopped somewhere."

Trent laughed, "First off, no crime happens in this town while the farmer's market is going on. Second, why would I leave free pie?"

"Good point."

Trent liked the way she smiled with one side of her mouth.

"Still here, rookie?" Greggs said, patting Trent's back.

He had gone home and changed out of his uniform and looked less intimidating with jeans and a golf shirt on.

"Yes sir, all thirty minutes, and they gave me pie."

"They bribed you with pie, huh?"

"You were right sir. It's the best pie I've had."

"In that case," Greggs clapped his hands together,

"can you take a cherry pie to Mrs. Wilson?"

"Of course, Sir."

Lexy began wrapping up the pie.

"Suck up," she teased under her breath.

Trent took the box and patted Bones on the head.

"Thank you for the samples, Mrs. Greggs. It was nice meeting you, Lexy."

Trent walked back to his patrol car making a mental note to pick up one of Lexy's books to read.

Khunda

Chapter Three

ater that night Lexy stepped into her cottage, tossing her keys onto the bookshelf next to the door. Bones brushed past her and went straight to his water dish. He began sloping water not only into his mouth, but all over the floor.

"You're cleaning that up," she said, dropping her bag onto the stool in front of the kitchen counter with one hand and pushing the tab on her electric kettle with the other. Her house was a small, two bedroom cottage she had built two years earlier. One day she figured she could add onto it if her family grew. But for now, it was the perfect size for her and Bones.

Lexy grabbed her favorite mug with the moon's phases on it and turned to Bones. "So, do you feel like getting crazy tonight?"

He raised his snout, dripping with water.

Lexy picked a Ginger Jasmine tea bag from the box, opened it and dropped it into the mug.

"How about I write and you plop down wherever you want and sleep off all the treats you've had?" She laughed at Bones wagging his tail like crazy.

"I'll take that as a yes. How about listening to our rock out playlist?"

Bones sat next to his food dish as she grabbed her laptop out of her bag and turned on some music. The Star Trek theme song played as Lexy filled Bones' dish. He licked her nose in gratitude. After pouring her tea and picking a snack out of the pantry she sat down at her desk, tucking her legs beneath her and looking out the glass doors leading into the backyard. The sun was beginning to sink behind the mountains and the sky was a wash of soft pinks and yellows. Lexy sipped her tea, slightly burning the tip of her tongue.

In space, she found it difficult to find time to write, but while on Earth, she was able to sit for days without interruption. She grew up feeling like her heart was split in two, half on Earth and half in space. The mountains were an ideal place for the jump ship to pick her up. If, by chance, someone did see strange lights, her aunt and uncle helped downplay any claims of sightings in the nearby towns.

She turned her chair to face the desk. On the

wall in front of her was a push-pin board she used to keep inspired. She'd pin images, quotes or anything she wanted to manifest to the board. She reached over the desk and ran her finger along the edge of an image of three stars. These stars represented Lexy's hopes of one day becoming the first Earthling to rank as a three-star Captain.

Shaking her head to clear it, she took a deep breath and opened the file containing her new manuscript. She started typing and only stopped to refill her cup or let Bones out. The night outside grew darker. The sky turned into a black backdrop dotted with specks of light. She was typing the end of a chapter when a beeping noise came from a small device sitting on the kitchen counter.

The one inch, dark gray box could have been easily overlooked, and Lexy never would have heard the beeping over the music, but the small holographic figure that projected from the device into her living room caught her attention. The figure would have seemed strange to anyone else because it was three and a half feet tall with a reptilian tail. Lexy was raised around beings like this one since her parents had worked for the CTA as intergalactic transporters. They were killed when their ship was attacked by mercenaries. When Lexy's aunt and uncle took her in they already knew about the existence of aliens. Her parents had told them, asking them to keep it a secret.

The image cleared his throat, "Director Ameran

of Capital Transport Agency sending a message to Captain Greggs of the Khunda transport ship," he said, waiting patiently for a reply as Lexy jumped up, turned off the music and pulled her hair into a ponytail.

"Captain Greggs accepts the message," Lexy replied.

The figure gave a slight bow and phased out, replaced by the figure of an older woman in an emerald green pantsuit which went perfectly with her blue skin and the black hair pulled into a tight bun at the base of her neck.

"Director, I hope you are doing well," Lexy said, giving the hologram a smile.

"I have told you a million times, when it is just you and I, you can call me Ameran," the woman said giving Lexy a warm smile.

Lexy was one of the few people who had a close relationship with the Director. Her mother and Ameran had grown up together. When Lexy's parents died, Ameran kept an eye out for Lexy.

"I am fine. And you?"

"Wonderful," Lexy clasped her hands behind her back.

"All patched up from the last mission, I hope," Ameran said, looking around the living room.

Lexy stared at her sock covered feet so Ameran couldn't see her cheeks redden.

"Yes ma'am," she said, still embarrassed that their last mission hadn't gone as planned, and the Khunda needed a lot of repairs. "Thank you. Just so you know, the mercenaries attacked us first. I think Z and I handled -"

The director held her hand up to stop Lexy.

"I read your report and you are not to blame." She smoothed her suit and continued, "I am well aware that the Royal Galaxies have become increasingly dangerous which means we are experiencing a shortage of adequate security personnel." Ameran waved her hand at the thought. "Lexy, I have a mission for you and this one is a very important. The Chancellor of the Royal Selection Committee paid a visit to my office, in person, to request my best crew for a transport. The cargo will be a member of the Royals. I have chosen you. Even with all the repairs to the Khunda the CTA had to fund, you are the Captain I trust to do whatever it takes to keep a Royal safe." she said.

Amaran tapped a small tablet that was handed to her from an unseen source, "We don't have all of the details as of yet, but this is going to be a high profile transport with all eyes on you." She stared at Lexy pointedly, "The CTA needs this one. This will help our standing with the committee. Can I count on you as I counted on your parents?"

Lexy hoped she'd heard incorrectly. "Seriously?" Lexy asked.

Ameran shifted in confusion.

Lexy took a breath to calm herself. ”I'm sorry, I just can't believe it. You want me and Z to transport a Royal while all of the royal planets are watching?” Lexy pinched the bridge of her nose, "Is this a low level royal? Maybe one they deem expendable?"

Ameran began tapping on the tablet again, ignoring Lexy's comments. “I knew I could count on you. I will send Z to pick you up tomorrow evening and have preliminary plans sent to you. Come straight to my office as soon as you get here so I can fill you in on anything new.”

Lexy forced a grin. "Yes, ma'am.”

Ameran smiled back at Lexy and then disappeared. The red light on the device faded.

Letting out a long breath, she slid her hands down her face.

“Why would she pick us? We're shit magnets.”

The thought of having a royal on her ship made her stomach ache. Her mind was racing through all the possible outcomes of this mission. Each of them ended in her losing her ship and even her enlightened status, causing her to spend the rest of her life on Earth with no way to contact her friends and family, including her best-friend Z and any other non-humanoid. These were people she grew up with, some even knew her parents. The edges of her eyes began to burn as tears formed. Lexy forced her eyes closed, counting backward from ten. It'll be OK. She won't send us out there without security. Besides, Z and I have always survived. Balling her hands into fists, she stood straighter in determination.

I will make sure this mission is a success.

Lexy cleaned up her mess and headed to her bedroom. She gave a slight whistle when she reached the door and Bones bounded into the room, curling up on the corner of the bed. Lexy picked up a black backpack and put a few things into it, including her laptop. She would have a lot of downtime on a Royal transport; at least she could work on her next book. Looking around the untidy room she figured that was all she was going to need. It's just a transport, a couple of days, tops.

Lexy dug through a drawer for a clean set of PJs, changed, brushed her teeth and slipped under the covers, trying not to disturb Bones who was already snoring. Staring at the glow-in-the-dark stars littered across the ceiling, she remembered they'd been in every bedroom she'd ever had. In her childhood home, her mother put them, in the correct constellations, then May and Greggs helped her stick them all over her room when she moved in with them. As time passed, she'd studied the night sky to make sure she knew exactly where to put them when she moved into her first place. She reached down to pet Bones on the head before drifting into a dreamless sleep.

The sun woke Lexy. She rolled onto her side and looked out the window thinking about what life would be like if her parents were still alive. Most mornings were filled with thoughts of them. Would she be a crew member of their ship? Would family meals be spent talking about successful missions and laughing about mishaps during others? She rolled onto her back and for a split-second Trent's face entered her mind. She didn't need any male distractions. Growling a bit at the thought, she slid out of bed and started the shower. Bones raised his head and then lowered it back to the sheets with a huff when he realized she wasn't getting up to fill his food bowl..

After she showered, Lexy grabbed an apple, filled Bone's dish and collected any items she hadn't packed the night before. Looking at her phone, she realized she was running late.

"Damn!"

Lexy tossed her bag in the back seat of her SUV. Jumping in the driver's seat, she started it and began pulling out of the driveway. Slamming on the breaks she leaned over the passenger's side and pushed the door open.

"Bones let's go!"

Bones, still sitting on the side of the driveway, barked a reply.

"I'm sorry, now get in the car," Lexy said.

Bones hopped onto the seat and let out a puff of

air in annoyance. The ride was quiet as they made their way down the mountain. After her first three books, Lexy bought a couple of acres and built the one-bedroom cottage. She planned to build onto it if there was ever a need to, but for now, it was the perfect size for her and Bones.

Just a few minutes later the pair entered the kitchen of her aunt and uncle's house. Bones, refusing to forgive Lexy for almost forgetting him, trotted into the living room and lay on the couch next to Greggs.

"What did you do to upset him?" May asked.

"I'm human, that's what I did," Lexy said.

Lexy hugged May, inhaling her rose petal perfume.

"Can I ask you for a favor?" Lexy asked, letting go of May. She walked around the island and dipped her finger into the bowl of chocolate pudding.

May tried to slap her hand away.

"What is it, Lex?" May asked.

"I have an assignment starting tonight. Can you watch Bones for a couple of days?"

"Of course, you know we will!" May said, leaning forward to look into the living room. "Besides it looks like he and your uncle are doing their male bonding."

Lexy looked around the corner to find Bones helping Greggs finish off a plate of sausages.

"Just so you know, he's sitting in the back seat

with you!" Lexy raised her eyebrows as her uncle met her eyes, his cheeks burning red.

"Oops!" Greggs said.

Lexy giggled, turning to look at May as she pressed pie dough into the pans. She knew how lucky she was to have May and Greggs in her life. The thought of where she would be if they hadn't taken her in was terrifying. They were known as Enlightened Earthlings and came from long lineages of families who helped cover up the existence of aliens. Lexy's parents were killed on a mission when she was fifteen. They had worked for the CTA transporting high profile clients on the ship, Andreia. It was rare for the CTA to hire Earthlings at that time, but her mother was half Royal and best friends with Ameran, whose father was the Director of the CTA.

Lexy grabbed a spoon from the drawer and scooped up some of the chocolate pudding. As she ate it she remembered the story of how her parents met at the Royal Intergalactic Academy and fell madly in love. Her mother was studying flight Security, while her father was going through the Captain's program. They worked on separate ships for years in the Royal Guard, eventually proving themselves to Ameran's father, who allowed them to join the CTA. They were the first Earthlings in the CTA. They were paired with a pilot, Z's father, and went on to become one of the best crews at the CTA until they were attacked in the

Cancer Constellation. Z's father barely survived. The Royal Guard investigated the attack, concluding that rebels from the Draco constellation were to blame. Lexy was assured by Ameran's father that the Royal Council had hunted down and killed the attackers.

Any chance of relaxing was pushed out of Lexy's mind by the morning deliveries. They packaged and loaded several pies into May's SUV. After checking to make sure they had everything, they piled into the car. Greggs sat in the back with Bones, and Lexy took the passenger seat. May pulled out of the gravel driveway and filled the ride with gossip about women in the town. Lexy let her aunt talk while she checked the few details available on the CTA tablet. Symbols flashed across the screen. As a part of her Academy curriculum, she had to learn a number of languages. This came in handy when her uncle's prying eyes wandered to the strange characters that held her flight plan and itinerary.

"So, you're off to work…again?"

Shrugging, Lexy turned off the tablet.

 "Yeah. Political shit."

The tap across the back of her head let her know that May had been listening.

"Ladies do not cuss!"

"Sorry, May."

Lexy peeked over her shoulder just in time to see

Greggs cover a laugh.

"Don't think I don't hear you, Mister, I know who taught her those words" May met his eyes in the mirror, winking at him in the reflection.

"You will be safe though, right?" May stopped at a red light, her hand on Lexy's knee.

"Yes, I am always safe," but she looked away before May could read her expression.

They pulled into a parking space on Central Avenue. Most of the local restaurants bought May's pies for their dessert menus.So, twice a week, May, Greggs and sometimes Lexy would deliver the orders before the restaurants opened. Lexy got out and stretched while Greggs walked behind the SUV, opened the back and began sorting through pie boxes. It was still early, only a few people were walking around. Lexy leaned against the side of the car,

"Anyone want coffee?"

"You know that stuff will stunt your growth?"

This was May's go-to remark when it came to coffee.

"I'm thirty years old, I think it will affect my height all that much at this point," She looked at Greggs.

"Small, two sugars," Greggs said.

May mumbled under her breath as Lexy stepped to the curb. Bones decided to follow her down the sidewalk. He stopped to sniff a flower pot as Lexy scratched his head and entered the cafe. She flipped through emails on her phone as she stood in line.

"Your usual?" Lexy looked up to see Sally smiling at her.

"Please, and my uncle's as well."

She nodded as Lexy handed her a card.

Lexy moved to the other side of the counter as another customer ordered. She began answering an email from her agent when she heard Sally's voice change.

"Hi Trent, would you like your usual?"

Lexy looked up from her phone, her eyes meeting Trent's. He smiled. She looked back at her phone, hoping he couldn't tell that her pulse had sped up.

"How was your first night shift?" Sally asked

Lexy rolled her eyes, "Oh please," she mumbled.

Trying to focus on the words she was typing, she turned slightly, facing the counter. It didn't help.

"You should have been there last night. Steve had too much to drink and began singing Dancing Queen," Sally giggled.

Lexy snorted a little too loudly. Glancing up she noticed Sally and Trent were staring at her. Her cheeks began to burn. Sally looked at Lexy, annoyed.

Lexy figured she should say something to explain her outburst. "I just meant that Steve has been doing that since high school. The logic that Trent actually missed something worth seeing is misguided…" She was rambling. Sally kept staring at her and Trent was smirking. Feeling the pressure of their eyes she continued, "Sorry, I just meant that…I'm going to shut up now because my coffee is ready."

She slid her phone into her back pocket and picked up the cups. Lexy noticed that Steve had made her coffee. "Thanks, Steve." she squeaked.

Steve crossed his arms and glared at her. He had heard her comments as well. Heat filled her face. *What is wrong with me?*

She stopped at the condiment table to add sugar to Gregg's cup and cinnamon to her cappuccino. Trent set his cup down next to hers. He reached for the sugar and added some to his cup. Lexy glanced up at him. He was smiling. *Annoying*.

"Are you still laughing?" she asked.

"No, ma'am," he replied.

"Don't 'ma'am me."

Lexy replaced the lids on the cups and walked to the door. Before she reached it, Trent rushed past her and held the door open for her.

"Thanks," she mumbled.

"You two must be friends," Trent said, keeping pace with her as he sipped his coffee.

Lexy shrugged. She never understood what Sally and her friends saw in spending their evenings at the local bars.

Bones pushed his way between them and let Trent scratch between his ears.

"Hey buddy, long time no see."

May was walking their way, carrying pie boxes up to her nose. Trent set his cup down on someone's hood and jogged up to her, taking the boxes. They walked into a restaurant, chatting. Lexy looked around, hoping the owner of the truck Trent set his coffee on wasn't around. She readjusted her grip on the coffee cups in her hands to add Trent's to them.

"Got it!" Bones wagged his tail. "Thanks for the help," she said sarcastically, but with a smile.

Lexy walked to May's car and set the cups on the hood. She leaned her hip against the car, sipping her coffee. The band on her arm vibrated. Setting her cup down she began swiping her finger across the band. Lexy read a list of items that had been ordered for the transport.

"She ordered what?!?"

She slapped her hand over her mouth and pulled her sleeve down over her band.

"Something wrong?"

Lexy jumped, and turned around. May was stepping off the curb.

"Maybe you shouldn't check your messages until you get to work."

May patted her shoulder and walked to the back of her car. Trent was crouched next to Bones, scratching him under the collar. Lexy cleared her throat.

"Here's your coffee. Don't want to keep you from your day."

May's head popped around the car.

"Lexy dear, Trent offered to help deliver the pies this morning."

"Great."

She finished her coffee and tossed the cup into the trash can. Trent followed her to the back of the SUV.

"What? You don't need any help?" he asked.

May shoved a stack of boxes into Lexy's arms before she could answer.

"Trent, dear, don't mind Lexy. She's just in a mood," May explained.

"Sorry to hear that," he said, winking at her over the stack of boxes he had picked up.

"Those are going to the brewing company," May said, pointing down the street.

They walked across the street in silence. Bones had decided to stay with May, so Lexy didn't have anyone to run interference for her. Trent seemed to find the silence discomforting.

"So, May said you were heading out of town for work. Anything fun?"

"Not this time," Lexy said flatly.

Trent stopped, cocking his head to one side. "Did I do something?" he asked.

Lexy stopped and faced him. "No, why?"

"You've been snappy since we got coffee," he said.

Lexy sighed, "We need to get these pies to the restaurant."

"Not until you answer me," Trent said, keeping eye contact.

Lexy wanted to look away but she couldn't. His eyes were locked onto hers. She knew her face was turning red and heat began to flood her body.

"I'm just stressed. I have an important meeting and…" her voice trailed off.

"You're mad at me because of it?" Trent asked.

"No, I'm not mad at you. Look, can we walk and talk, because not all of us do push-ups for shits-and-giggles?"

Trent began walking again. "Ok, so work is stressing you out. Can't you just take a break?"

"Ha," Lexy adjusted her grip on the boxes, "and what would I do?"

"What do you like to do? Besides work?"

"Skate, go trail riding or hiking when it's warm."

She surprised herself with how open she was with

Trent. Most people only got to hear what May and Greggs told them.

"Ice skating?" Trent asked, a shocked look on his face.

"Yes, ice skating. Why?" Lexy asked.

"I play hockey. We should go skate sometime." He looked intently at the sidewalk in front of him.

Is he asking me on a date?

They stopped in front of the doors to the brewery.

"Uh- sure."

Lexy lightly kicked the bottom of the door. Trent was smiling at her when Todd, the manager, let them in. Lexy introduced Trent to the morning staff and after they unloaded the pies they walked back to the car, talking about how they got into skating. When all the pies were delivered Trent excused himself, explaining to May he had to get ready for work.

"We have to have you over for dinner to thank you for your help," May said as she gave him a hug before climbing into the driver's seat.

Greggs shook Trent's hand and then slid into the backseat next with Bones.

"Thanks for the help," Lexy said, shaking Trent's hand.

He kept her from pulling her hand back.

"Let me know when you get back from your

work trip and I'll take you up on skating and dinner," Trent said.

"I don't remember dinner being included," Lexy exclaimed.

Trent released her hand and jogged across the street. Lexy watched him, not sure if he had heard her.

"I don't remember agreeing to dinner!" she yelled after him. What nerve! Mental note: handle that when I get back.

Khunda

Chapter Four

Trent arrived at the station just in time to wake Officer Sims from his nap.

"Man, it has been a sleeper of a day. Williams and Anderson are on a call. Apparently, a party at the lodge got out of hand tonight and someone got a little flirty with a waitress. His wife found out and all hell broke loose," he explained, stretching in his chair.

Trent flipped through the contents of his mailbox, "Do they need backup?"

"Nah, it's just an argument. Sounds like they just need some couples therapy, but if you get bored easily, I'm sure you could check it out."

Sims pulled on his jacket.

"Have a good night, Trent," he said, giving Trent a nod.

Trent sat at his desk staring at the radio. He wasn't the type to just sit around, so told Peggy, the town dispatcher, he was going to see if the guys needed any help. He offered to pick her up something to eat but she shook her head and continued knitting. He got in the patrol car and pulled out onto the dark street heading toward the ski lodge at the edge of the lake. When he arrived and walked into the lobby the wife was crying hysterically while her husband talked to Anderson. Williams stood near the wife with a look that said he hadn't had much experience with crying women. Trent walked up to the check-in desk where a young man, named Michael according to his manager's name tag, looked panicked.

"Hi, I'm Officer Trent."

"Hi," he shook Trent's hand.

"Do you know how long this is going to take? There's a business dinner here ending soon and dozens of guests will be passing through here. I would rather them not see the police and a hysterical woman."

"Let me check with them and I'll find out for you."

Michael's shoulders relaxed just a bit as Trent walked up to Williams.

"You have a very nervous manager over there," he said with a nod aimed at the front desk.

Williams looked over Trent's shoulder.

"He's in luck. These two are heading back to their room as soon as Anderson is done talking to the husband."

Trent nodded. He looked around and found a box of tissues sitting on a table. He grabbed it and set it next to the wife.

"Thank you," she squeaked out between sobs.

Trent gave her a smile. A couple of minutes later the couple headed to the elevators, arm-in-arm. Anderson updated the manager and the officers headed out to the parking lot.

They were standing by the cars talking about where to stop for dinner when a call came over the radio. Someone was claiming they'd seen strange lights on Big Mountain. They all agreed to drive in separate directions around the mountain to check it out.

"Probably a bunch of kids playing around," Anderson said, getting into his car.

Trent drove up the mountainside with the windows rolled down, enjoying the brisk fall air. The only sound was the air rushing past his car. There were no gunshots, no threat of car bombs, and no RPGs. Trent had loved being a soldier, and no one could tell him otherwise, but from time-to-time he woke up in the middle of the night from the nightmares. He knew he wasn't the only soldier to suffer from them.

They all started out the same; he was walking down a random street minding his own business and the next thing he knew he heard a child crying. He'd search for the child under cars, around trees and even climb through windows, yet he never found where the crying was coming from. The further he walked down the road looking for the child the more the streets began to look like the war-torn country he'd fought to protect. The buildings were more riddled with bullet holes, smoke began rising in the distance, and the crying got louder. When the noise, smoke, and destruction became too much to bear, he'd cover his ears, close his eyes and yell, "STOP!", and everything did. He'd open his eyes to find himself in a dark room, a holding cell. The small space is where many of his friends were tortured. Down the hall just passed the closed door of this cold dark cell he could hear footsteps. They were coming for him, he knew they were. He was next; it was time for his pain. The steps got closer, louder, until they stopped at the door. Trent felt the cold hardness of the wall pressing into his back. Keys jiggled, the lock clicked, and then the door swung open. All Trent could see was a bright light. Then he'd wake up and shoot out of bed, breathing heavy; heart racing, eyes darting around the room until he knew where he was and that it was only a dream. This is why he hated the night. This is why he moved so far from home and big cities. He needed the quiet.

He pulled the patrol car into an empty parking spot off to one side of the Hellroaring Saloon, the only restaurant open at the top of the slopes during the offseason.

He turned off the car, looking around the lot to make sure he hadn't missed a car sitting somewhere in the shadows. Nope, nothing here. Through the bank of windows on the side of the saloon he could see a woman talking to Fred, the manager. He leaned forward to get a better look. The woman looked familiar. Trent got out of the car, walking toward the door. He noticed the customer had long dark hair in a braid down the middle of her back. She slid a backpack on; one Trent had seen before. It was Lexy.

What was she doing out here, without her car … without Bones?

She said something to Fred and gave him a hug. Trent watched as she grabbed a plastic bag sitting on the counter, but instead of heading toward the exit, she walked into the kitchen. Something was off.

Adjusting his duty belt, Trent opened the door and walked toward the manager. Fred seemed shocked to see him, but quickly recovered.

"Hello Officer Trent, you working tonight?" he asked.

"Yes, where did Lexy go?" Trent responded.

Fred's face returned to wearing a look of shock.

"You must be mistaken. I have been alone all night," he lied, "We get most of our business in the winter."

Trent was not about to play games.

"I'm going to back there, ok?"

He pointed to the door Lexy disappeared through.

"You have a good night," Trent called over his shoulder.

The man stuttered as he rushed after Trent, but Trent was faster. He burst through the door to the kitchen. The kitchen was empty except for the surprised cook sitting just inside the door. Trent nodded to him and looked for an exit door. She had to have gone out the back. Trent glanced around one last time to make sure he hadn't overlooked any hiding places around the meal prep area. He pushed through the exit door. It closed silently behind him. Trent paused as his eyes adjusted to the darkness. He stood at the back entrance of the building. To his left he could make out the large dumpster; he knew it was green because all of them were green. To his right a small red truck that looked as if it had seen better days sat under the only light. Trent assumed it belonged to Fred.

The snap of a twig jerked his attention to the woods spreading out in front of him. He stepped forward a bit and then stopped again, his foot on the curb that bordered the grass leading into the woods on one side and the parking lot on the other. He squinted to see if he could make out a figure. Then there was another snap of a twig just beyond the first. Trent jumped into action; hand on his Glock out of habit. He ran through bushes, ducking under tree branches and dodging fallen debris, thinking something had to be wrong. There is no reason anyone should be in the cold woods, in the dark, this far from town. The top of a mountain was no place to be wandering around. They could get lost or attacked by wild animals. Trent was sure something wasn't right.

He leapt off the curb and began following the direction of the snapped twig. In the distance ahead he made out a shadow, but how could that be? It was a New Moon. There shouldn't be any light out here. Just as he thought this, the light in front of the figure got brighter, while a strange humming noise became louder. The hum seemed to turn off his hearing. He couldn't hear the wind, or Fred calling his name from the restaurant. As Trent got closer, he could make out her shape. Yep, it was Lexy. He began to run faster. The hum silenced his steps. He was thankful the ground was dry so he had less chance of slipping. He was so close now that he slowed to a light jog. He didn't want to startle Lexy, or anyone else who might be out here. Could that be the reason she was wandering through the woods among the shadows? Was she meeting someone? Trent stepped up to a thick tree on the edge of the clearing Lexy was walking into. The light brightened. In the same instant, she disappeared.

He focused on the last spot he'd seen her; his heart beginning to race. He opened his mouth to call out to her, but as his eyes adjusted to the light, he noticed something. His jaw dropped in surprise and adrenaline flooded his bloodstream when he realized what sat in the center of the clearing. The large object the size of a plane, but not like any plane he'd ever seen. The shape was more of a triangle with rounded corners. The outside was a dark gray metal covered with symbols Trent had never seen before. His heart hammered harder now. Nothing in his life had prepared him for this.

Where did she go? What do I do?

Trent's thoughts bounced around in his head with no clarity. Then in an instant they stopped and his Army training took over. He took a deep breath to steady himself, squared his shoulders and ran to the door Lexy had vanished into. The hum was coming from under the silver and black metal. The ramp leading into the fading light shifted, rising slowly. He used his right leg to push off and then launched himself forward, hurtling like a missile into the craft's opening, which was becoming smaller by the second. He fell hard onto his knees inside the door, and then tumbled in an awkward landing from the forward momentum. Pain shot up his legs and he winced, breathing into it, waiting for the needle-like jabs to subside. Behind him the door closed, a red light above his head flashed as an alarm echoed off the walls around him.

The pain caused his vision to blur around the edges as he looked up to take in the room. He didn't see Lexy, but her bag sat on a chair to his left. He shook his head in an attempt to clear his mind. It took all his strength to get to his feet. He staggered to the wall on his right; his legs pulsing with pain. *Next time I have to remember to try the superhero landing.*

The wall was lined with pipes; each had strange symbols on them. He grabbed one to steady himself just as a low rumble shook the floor of the craft. It felt like aircraft turbulence. He saw three doors at the end of the walkway and stumbled to the one on his right where the pipes disappeared into. It slid open as he approached. The floor jolted and he lost his balance, falling into a stack of boxes just inside the door, which closed behind him.

"Son of a bi-"

Regaining his footing he rushed to open the door, but it wouldn't budge. His palms started sweating as he realized he was stuck in the dark on a strange craft.

Night shift sucks.

Khunda

Chapter Five

A board the jump ship, Lexy rushed into the cockpit and pushed the button on the wall. The door behind her slid closed as she set the plastic bag in a chair in front of the control console. She began pressing several buttons.

"Welcome aboard Captain," the Khunda's automated voice welcomed. "Would your guest-"

"Lex!" Z, the Khunda's pilot and Lexy's best friend took control of the com. "We're running late. What the hell were you doing? Washing your hair?" Z's voice was loud, but the rock music he had playing was louder.

"Khunda, turn off the music." The small space went silent. "That's better. First off, I'm two minutes late and second, why did you send the jump ship with its lights on? Someone had to have seen it land," Lexy scolded.

"Uh- crap I knew I forgot something."

Lexy could hear Z moving around.

"Whatever. I'm heading up, send me the coordinates."

Lexy sat down and tapped away on the console. The small ship jumped into motion. Trees fell out of view and were replaced with the evening sky. The small ship's engine hummed louder. Lexy pressed back into her chair as the ship jolted into top speed, leaving the Earth's atmosphere.

Z's hologram face popped up on the edge of the console. "I parked it on the far side this time so watch your temps," he warned.

"Will do. Hey, did the Director send any more info on this mission?" she asked, sliding her arms into the CTA jacket she'd left on the chair.

Z shook his head. "Nope. Why do you think she gave it to us?"

Lexy pushed the top of the plastic bag down so Z couldn't see it.

"Don't know. She's sending us, so I'm assuming it's no one important."

"You know you're her golden child, right?" Z teased.

"Shut it," Lexy warned. "Yeah, she took me under her wing when my parents died, but our work should speak for itself. If we do a good job on this it could get us a little closer to my third star and your senior pilot promotions. So that means no fucking around, right?" her eyes narrowed as she took in Z's face.

Z shrugged, "What? It's not always my fault."

"Point being, we have to be on the same page with this," she said.

"I know."

Lexy looked out into the blackness of space. The right side of her screen was filled with the gray, dusty landscape of the moon.

"I'm almost there. Warm up the engines. Maybe we can make up the two minutes I was late," Lexy teased, smiling at Z who rolled his eyes.

"Will do, Captain." Z's face disappeared.

"Khunda, coming in to dock, please open the cargo bay."

"Yes, Captain," Khunda answered.

The Khunda sat silently in the shadow of a lunar mountain range. Lexy smiled as the jump ship eased closer.

She steered the ship into the bay and when it settled into its berth, she snatched the bag next to her and exited the cockpit into the jump ship's common space. She picked up her backpack on her way to the now open ramp. The bay reminded her of a military hanger. The jump ship was tucked along the back wall and several large boxes were stacked to the side, filled with emergency supplies that, thankfully, they hadn't had to use yet.

Lexy glanced at the larger, open cargo ramp facing the moon's surface. She could see the slight twinkle of the force field that separated her from the Moon's surface.

Thank god for advanced technology.

She took the stairs two at a time and then swiped the band on her left wrist across the keypad to open the elevator doors. Lexy stepped in and pressed a symbol on the wall. A soft hum came from somewhere above her head as the elevator took her to the top floor. Seconds later a chime rang out just before the doors slid open. She stepped into motion and walked along a curved hallway. On one side was a series of constellations spread out nicely against the backdrop of a cream-colored wall. The other side of the hall was open, with a waist high railing overlooking the common room that lay a level below. The hall curved in a large circle, and to her right, just a few feet away, was the bridge. The door opened as Lexy approached, revealing a space that felt more like home to her than an office. In the center was a glass-like table that curved slightly on the ends, making it look like a crescent moon. Two chairs sat behind the table, facing a massive window that took up most of the front wall. As her eyes slide across the length of the window, she took in the small white lights that she knew were the same stars they were headed toward.

Lexy took in the rest of the room she knew by heart. To her left another glass-like counter was fixed to the wall, its surface was just like a keyboard except the characters would be alien to anyone who wasn't familiar with the Orion language. Above the keyboard was another glass surface that flashed with constellations and planets. This was the navigation console. To her right, the three black, high-back chairs lining the back wall were used to control the Khunda's advanced weaponry systems. The headrests picked up on the user's thoughts, allowing them to control the weapons with pinpoint accuracy. It was the most advanced system in the fleet.

Breathing in deeply, Lexy walked to the center console. She dropped into the unoccupied chair and turned to Z.

"I got you a gift," she said.

Z's almond eyes lit up, "Gimme gimme gimme," he said, reaching for the bag like a child.

She placed the plastic bag in his outstretched hands.

"I hope the old man didn't forget the Zebra cakes… Ah here they are. I love Fred; that man is a life saver!"

Z ripped open the box with his small grey hand and set the bag on the floor.

Lexy rolled her eyes. Since she had known Z

their whole lives, she was used to his ridiculous taste buds and slightly jealous of his high metabolism.

"Khunda, let's take off and head to the first jump station," she called out.

"Yes, Captain," the Khunda answered.

Trent had been searching for another way out of the dark room filled with large metal boxes covered in strange symbols he couldn't make heads or tails of. He squeezed his way through the maze of boxes only to find there were no other doors. The floor jolted again. Trent sucked in his breath, listening for any signs of movement. Suddenly the door slid open with a swooshing sound. He rushed toward the door, smacking his hip on the last box as he passed it, and then slid to a stop in the walkway.

Why did the door open? I'm getting the hell out of here before something else closes.

He sped down the ramp he had jumped through earlier, looking back just to make sure the craft was still there.

Ok, so that was real. But what exactly is it?

Trent looked around, taking in the larger cargo space he was in now. Boxes, similar to the ones in the room, were stacked to the left of a set of stairs leading up to the elevator doors. As he scanned the bay, his jaw fell open. In front of him was an open ramp, this one bigger than the one he just walked out of. The land outside was gray, like ash. Surveying the landscape his mind began to race.

Where on Earth am I?

He moved closer, and could see the sky covered in white dots.

Stars?

There were so many he could never count them all. As he neared the ramp some of the dots moved with incredible speed and some even suddenly disappeared. The biggest surprise was a large sphere he'd only seen in images taken at vast distances. Earth.

"What. The. Fuck." He exhaled.

The floor began to hum and the lights in the bay went out. He slid his hands along the wall to his right. A faint light from outside the door began to dim, telling him the massive ramp was closing. His heart pounded in his chest harder than he'd ever felt in his life.

Should I jump out?

The floor jumped and Trent fell, slamming his head against a pipe. His body fell to the ground with a thud and his vision went black.

Khunda

Chapter Six

L exy propped her feet up on the console.

"So, did you look through our mission report? Or were you too busy with the woman of the week?" she asked.

"Wha- wo-an oph uh eek?"

Z beamed through his mouthful of cake. Seeing Lexy's disapproving glance, he swallowed hard and wiped his mouth with the back of his hand.

"Lex, you know there are no other women in my life but you and the Khunda," Z answered, a sly smile spread across his face.

"Oh, we both know they don't have to be in your life for you to bang them," Lexy giggled. "Pass me an apple."

Z handed her one and mumbled under his breath,

"At least I'm not the one who screwed Captain fancy pants."

Lexy was appalled that Z would bring THAT up… again.

"Look, I was drunk and we were stuck at that fuel station for three days! You were off bumping uglies with those hybrid whores. Oh God, I'm going to vomit if we keep talking about this."

Lexy rolled her eyes and focused on her apple.

"Fine," Z huffed, shoveling another cake into his mouth.

The room fell silent. Lexy began touching symbols on the glass with one hand while taking bites of the fruit with the other. Z mashed a small green light on the console in front of him. Music blared through unseen speakers.

"REALLY, Z! YOU KNOW I HATE THIS CRAP!" Lexy bellowed at him.

WHAT?!?! I CAN'T HEAR YOU, THE MUSIC IS TOO LOUD," he bellowed back, pointing to the ceiling with his middle finger.

Lexy couldn't help but laugh. She tossed the apple core at him. Z caught it and pressed the console again; silencing the jumbled mess of sound he called music.

"Captain," the Khunda chimed in, "we are approaching the Milky Way Galaxy jump station. I have sent them our jump approval documents. They are asking to speak with you. Shall I patch them through?"

Lexy and Z exchanged glances. The Agency's documents were usually enough, it was rare that a station would want to speak to the captain of one of their ships.

"Patch me through."

Lexy dropped her feet from the console as Z hid the box of cakes and brushed crumbs from his pants and the console in front of him. They both pretended to be thoroughly occupied as the screen changed to show a young man's face. His pointed ears and green skin told her he was a mixed species. The man looked to be in his mid-twenties, with short blonde hair and blue as the sky eyes. She was glad to see that the Guard was beginning to hire mixed candidates.

"Captain, this is Officer Thompson of the Royal Guard. I don't mean to interrupt, but I was looking at your documents and noticed your ship has the stage nine weapons systems. Any system above stage seven is subject to inspection--"

Lexy cut him off.

"Since when? This is a Silver level transport ship. If the Director hears about you invading my ship you will never find a job this side of the black," she snapped.

Officer Thompson looked down in an attempt to hide the red spreading across his cheeks. Another voice, somewhere off screen, captured his attention.

"She's the daughter of Jacob Greggs," the voice

said.

Officer Thompson's face changed in recognition, turning to a pale green. "I'm sorry to bother you ma'am. You may proceed."

With that the screen changed back to black space riddled with stars. Z broke the silence

"God, I love being your friend, do you know how much ass-"

"Z, just get us ready to jump," she said, tears pushing their way into her eyes before she dropped her head and tried to compose herself.

Lexy hated being reminded of her parents Their names brought back images of their funeral on Earth and the memorial in space. She was sixteen when their ship was attacked because of the cargo it held. She shook her head, scattering the memories. Since their death, Lexy had searched every report, every story and every account that related to their death. When she entered the captain's program at the intergalactic academy, she spent every spare minute searching the archives looking for a clue as to who murdered them. Nothing. Just as quickly as the attack ship arrived, it vanished. None of the survivors could identify the ship or its crew. To this day, her parent's murderers went unpunished forcing Lexy to give up hope of ever finding closure.

"Captain, we are ready to jump," Khunda's voice

was soothing, even over the speakers.

"Thank you, Khunda," Lexy responded, wiping away the tears.

"All systems ready?" Lexy asked, buckling herself in.

Z nodded. "Lex, I'm sorry I didn't-"

"Forget it Z, you didn't do anything wrong."

"Captain, you should ignore that ignorant, asswipe." The words sounded unnatural when delivered in Khunda's calm tone.

Lexy's jaw dropped open as she turned to Z, who stared straight ahead, his eyes twice their normal size.

"Did you teach her that?" Lexy asked.

"Define teach," Z said, meeting her eyes.

Lexy couldn't hold back the laughter. She doubled over, gripping her side.

"Just- go ahead- and- jump." She managed to choke out the words between laughing and gulping for air.

Z laughed with her, pressing several lights on the console.

The engines rumbled to life, their pitch getting higher.

"Jump in 3...2...1," Z slammed the gear to his left forward and the Khunda responded with a jolt.

The ship sped toward two metal crescent shapes. Electricity began to spark between them, the strikes jumping across the nearly seven mile gap powerfully enough to create a black spot in the center. Lexy knew this spot would grow and fill the space in the blink of an eye.

The large amounts of energy generated small wormholes in space, linking the constellations and making travel between them just a blink away.

Once the Khunda passed the checkpoint, the black spot grew to fill the space between the semicircles. Lexy pressed herself into the back of the chair, gripping the armrests. The front of the Khunda touched the black and before she could inhale the ship was sucked into the void. The next thing she knew, space was zooming past them. The walls of the ship hummed, giving only a hint of the speed they were traveling at. The jump only lasted a minute before they were spit out through an identical semicircular device and into the center of Orion's belt. A multitude of stars stretched out before them, ensuring even the most studied sailor would be lost in this piece the universe.

"Khunda has cleared the jump, Captain," Khunda declared with no further questionable language.

"Khunda, set a course for headquarters on Alpha Orion," Lexy said. She unfastened the seatbelt and stood to stretch her back. She clasped her hands behind her back and arched over backwards. Standing upright once again she let out a deep breath.

"Course set, Captain. We should arrive at Alpha

Orion in twenty minutes."

Lexy walked over and placed a hand on Z's shoulder, "Are you good? I need to put my stuff up."

"I'm good Lex," Z patted her hand.

She turned and walked out the door, stopping just long enough to grab the bag she'd tossed in the corner earlier. Turning right, she reached a door across from the elevator. A two inch thick nameplate sat at eye level with *Captain Greggs* etched into the metal. The door slid open as she approached. Lexy stepped in, taking in the room. It was just as she had left it. The rectangular main room included a small kitchen to her right, a couch across from the door, allowing whoever sat there a view out of the window that ran the length of the room. In front of it was a small coffee table and two more comfy chairs on either side. To her left, across from the door was a bay window with a high back chair. Lexy loved to sit and read and write here during their longer trips. Along the wall sat a floor-to-ceiling bookshelf stocked full of books from every planet they visited. Next to it a pair of French doors lay open, leading to the attached bedroom. She entered the room and tossed her bag on the closest chair and then turned toward the bedroom. She could use some cold water on her face.

The bed looked welcoming, but she struggled to resist the urge to just dive into the plush covers. She stayed on course, passing the large wardrobe which held mostly uniforms and went into the bathroom. Everything was sparkling and the linens were invitingly clean. The CTA was good at thorough cleanings whenever a ship was set to transport living cargo.

She let the cold water flow over her hands for a minute before splashing her face. Grabbing a towel, she patted her face dry and tossed the towel on the counter before walking back into the main room. Throwing a sideways glance at the couch as she passed, deciding that it, too, would be a good resting place when she had time. She grabbed a small bag of almonds from the counter, popped one in her mouth and returned to the bridge.

Z was bobbing his head to music blaring through the speakers. Lexy took her seat and he changed the song smirking. She didn't trust the look in his eyes, but began to laugh when the first notes of "Jump in the line" filled the room. She couldn't help but dance in her chair. Z stood and began to shimmy his hips. This made both of them laugh. She was grateful to have him as a pilot and friend; he always knew how to make her smile.

Ever since they were children they'd had a natural friendship. Their parents worked together on the same ship in the Royal Guard and then at the CTA, so Z and Lexy spent a lot of time together. Z always shared his toys, which were more advanced, with Lexy, and she let him borrow books she had finished reading. When Lexy's parents died,

Z was there. Not saying anything, but just there next to her. In the academy, she helped him study for his pilot's written exams and he helped with her languages classes. Z was the only pilot in the Guard that would take orders from an Earthling. So they were paired up during training and stationed on the outer edges of Royal space. When they both got offers to work for the CTA they made only one request; that they could work together. Quickly moving up the ranks, they become one of the Director's most trusted crews.

"Captain," Khunda said, interrupting Lexy's memories, "we are on course to dock at the CTA in five minutes."

"Thank you," Lexy yelled over the music.

Z shut off the music and began pressing buttons. They buckled themselves in.

"Go ahead and start pre-docking checks, Khunda."

Lexy let out a breath, relaxing back into her chair. She closed her eyes to review the little information they had about their mission, when her thoughts were interrupted by an alarm. Her eyes flew open.

"Captain, during docking scans I found that the being is not secured for landing." The Khunda's voice was calm. Lexy's bloodstream flooded with adrenaline.

Khunda

Chapter Seven

id I hear that right?

"What? The being? Where?" she demanded.

"The cargo bay, Captain," Khunda answered calmly.

Z and Lexy leapt from their chairs, raced through the door and down the hall. Stopping at a panel next to the elevator, Z pressed his hand against the wall and it shifted out of sight to reveal a weapon cabinet. They both grabbed small guns. Reaching over Z's head Lexy waved her hand in front of the elevator pad. The doors opened and the two stepped inside.

Lexy checked her weapon.

"You go invisible and cover me, ok?" she ordered.

Z nodded at her just before his small frame disappeared. The doors opened, revealing the large cargo bay. Slowly, Lexy stepped out onto the walkway that ran along the perimeter, her arms straight out in front of her, panning the pistol from right to left. The room was filled with the usual containers holding extra supplies. Behind them was a room full of tools and spare parts for the Khunda and the jump ship docked across from the bay door. She made her way down the stairs to get a better view. Halfway down she could see around a big box nestled next to the stairs. Her breath caught and she dropped her arms.

"Oh god; Trent."

She ran the last few steps to Trent's body, sensing Z leaping over the railing to her left. Dropping to her knees, she cupped his head in her hands. Dried blood marked the spot where he must have been hit by something.

"Crap Lex, who is this?" Z asked, reappearing next to her.

"He works with my uncle. Toss me the first aid bag."

She lowered his head onto the floor while checking for other injuries.

Z handed her a bag from the wall beside them.

"Like your uncle on Earth? How did he get here? How did you not see him get onboard?" Z asked.

Lexy frantically searched the bag for bandages and the portable scanner.

"Yes, Earth! I don't know and I don't care…" She slammed the bag down. "Where is the damn scanner?!"

Z quickly plunged his hand into the bag searching, while Lexy tore open the foil package filled with wipes. She cleaned away the blood to check the surface damage.

"Looks like a small lac."

"Ah ha!"

Z's hand shot into the air, the scanner in his four fingers.

Lexy took it, flipping the switch on the end. A thin blue light from one end to the other flickered on. She held the object above his heart and let go. It hovered inches above Trent's still body, a hologram spit out the top, an exact image of his body, except for a flashing red halo around his wound. Lexy flicked at the image like she was flipping the pages of a book, his image shifted through the layers on his body; muscle, nerves then to bones. She stopped, set his head lightly on the ground, moving to look at the area where the wound was from different angles.

"Good, skull isn't broken."

She flicked the image again to reveal his brain.

"No bleeding."

She let out all the air she was holding onto and dropped her head in relief.

"Good, he is alive. Now what are we going to do?" Z said, leaning against the cargo door. "The Director is going to lose her shit," he said, sliding down to sit at Trent's feet.

Lexy ignored him, dropping the scanner into the bag again and pulled out a tiny tube. Crushing the middle between her fingers, she pushed it up one of Trent's nostrils. His eyes shot open, taking in the world above him.

"Whoa, Trent. Don't get up. You hit your head," Lexy said and tossed the tube behind her with one hand. With the other, she held his shoulder down.

"I just had the weirdest dream," he said, "I was following you through the woods and-," he trailed off as his eyes fell on Z. Shooting up, he pressed his back into the wall before Lexy could stop him.

"What the fuck is that?!" Trent yelled.

Z stood, throwing his hands into the air.

"Well shit! Hi to you, too, asshole."

"Both of you stop. Z, go up to the bridge and make sure we don't hit anything. Trent, you need to stay calm and let me explain," she snapped.

Trent wasn't listening, his eyes were following Z. Lexy snapped her fingers in front of his face.

"Trent, how did you get on board?"

The elevator doors closed behind Z and Trent dropped his eyes to his lap, placing his hand to the bandage on his forehead.

"I followed you. I thought you were in trouble.

Where am I?"

Lexy sat back, crossing her legs in front of her

"You're aboard the transport ship, Khunda…The spaceship Khunda," Lexy said, drawing back in case the new information caused Trent to blow up.

Trent's eyes were wide as they scanned the open space. Lexy couldn't imagine what he was thinking.

This has got to be one hell of a shock.

The silence between them held more questions than either could process.

Sighing, Lexy climbed to her feet and extended her hand.

"Come on I'll show you."

Trent looked up at her hand, pausing before he took it. She pulled him to his feet and turned to walk back to the elevator. Lexy could hear his footsteps behind her. Once in the elevator she pushed the button for the auxiliary level, looking at Trent out of the corner of her eye. How was she going to explain this to someone who still thinks Earthlings are the only intelligent life forms? The doors opened, revealing a large kitchen to the left, tables and chairs in the center, two doors just beyond them and one door to the right. Lexy led the way to the door on the right. She could sense Trent taking everything in. She pushed the door open, motioning for Trent to go first. He stopped in the center of the oval room, staring through the window that took up the far wall.

The view always stunned Lexy, so she could only imagine how Trent was feeling. Billions of stars sparkled as ships of all sizes flew by. Space was a wonder to behold, especially around the capital planet, Alpha Orion.

"I know this is a lot, but I need to prepare you. We are about to dock at the CTA and you are going to see a lot of strange things," Lexy said, looking up at his face, trying to gauge his reaction. His eyes wide, taking it all in.

Sighing, his eyes met hers, "So, aliens are real?"

"Yes."

"We are in another galaxy?"

"No. We are in another constellation. Orion."

"That gray thing was an alien?"

"Yes...and his name is Z. It's short for Zefron. He is my best friend and the pilot of this ship. So, I would apologize if I were you."

"Oh."

Silence fell as they both looked out at the passing space. Lexy knew they had to go to the bridge.

"Are you ready to do this?" she asked.

"Sure."

They both turned and Lexy led the way back, to the elevator. They were silent, but she could tell his mind was swimming. The doors opened and Lexy walked into the hall, Trent in tow. He was looking over the railing at the common room below, only looking up when Lexy came to a stop in front of two sliding doors that opened onto the bridge. Walking to her chair, she sat facing Z. Trent shoved his hands into his pockets as Z faced Lexy.

"Is the stowaway caught up?"

"Yes he is. Are you going to be nice?"

"We'll see," Z said, facing the front.

Shrugging at Trent, Lexy motioned for him to take a seat at the navigation console. She had bigger fish to fry, like Ameran, and she was terrifying when she was mad. Not to mention the laws against allowing an unenlightened being to know about the existence of the royal planets. All three watched in silence as the Khunda floated silently in space.

"Captain, we are ready to dock," said Khundra's calm voice, which seemed to wake them from their thoughts. Z and Lexy buckled themselves in, while Trent fumbled around to find the buckles and then to fasten them correctly.

Lexy leaned forward pressing buttons, "Take us in."

Z's eyes focused on the small clear screen at the end of the console in front of him. The Khunda shifted so that the large screen looked out onto a lush looking planet. If it wasn't for the abundance of crafts flying around the planet, it could easily be mistaken for Earth.

Trent let out his breath. The view was stunning;

he still felt like he was in a dream.

Could that be my head injury? Aliens are real? I'm aboard a spacecraft? How hard did I hit my head?

He looked at the back of Lexy's head. She sat gripping the armrests, tense.

How long has she known about aliens? She said this was her ship?

Questions swirled around his head, making it hurt even more.

Lexy turned to look at him. Trent looked at the floor, unsure of what was going to happen when they landed on the planet. When he looked up she was facing front again. Instinct sent his gaze to the back of Z's head. Without turning, Z lifted his thin hand and what Trent could only guess was his middle finger.

This can't be real. I was just flicked off by an alien? I am about to land on another planet? I must have hit my head harder than I thought.

Trent's hand went to the bandage on his head as Z guided the ship into the planet's atmosphere. The ship shook slightly, forcing Trent to sit straight and press his back into the chair. Looking at the screen, the edges seem to be on fire. In seconds the view cleared and they drifted effortlessly toward a large city with white and clear buildings surrounded by clear water. Trent tilted his head.

Did I just see a whale?

As they glided closer, Trent noticed an island to the left of the city. In the center of the island a clear building stood several stories high, gardens twisted their way from the building to the water's edge where seven long docks shot out into the water. The Khunda eased toward the island.

"Preparing for docking, Captain," a soft woman's voice said, he didn't know where it came from.

Lexy reached forward, pressing a button Trent couldn't see.

"This is the Khunda, reporting for duty."

"Clear for dock 3, port 5. Welcome back, Khunda," said a woman's cheerful voice.

"Thank you, Alice." Lexy's tone gave the impression that the two knew each other.

They were hovering over one of the docks now, the ship at sea level. The landing was so soft that Trent thought they were still hovering until Lexy and Z undid their buckles. Facing Trent, Lexy dropped her hands to her sides.

"How are we going to explain this?"

Trent undid his own restraints, "I could stay here," he suggested.

"That won't work; they will have already scanned the ship. Ameran will know before we get to her office."

Lexy rubbed the back of her neck and said, "Let's get this over with."

She left bridge. Trent looked to Z for a sign of what to do next. Z motioned for Trent to follow Lexy. The three entered the elevator silently. Z pressed a symbol on the touchpad. Lexy had her arms crossed as the elevator hummed to life. Trent couldn't help but glance at Z. He was about four feet tall with light gray skin and large black eyes. Apparently aliens had visited Earth a few times.

Yep. I've lost my mind.

The doors opened and they were back in the cargo bay. Trent followed them down the stairs to the cargo door.

"Khunda, open the cargo door please." Lexy sounded apprehensive.

The doors opened slowly, and with every inch, Trent was amazed by the beauty that lay outside. He saw deep blue skies, the buzzing metropolis of the city on the larger island, and then the busy dock as the door settled open. There were people that looked just like him and Lexy, and then there were others. Some looked like Z and some were more alien. Tall, thin beings Trent guessed were over eight feet tall boarded the ship across from them. A group of knee high, furry creatures talked in a language Trent couldn't recognize, huddling over what looked like a see-through tablet.

Lexy and Z walked down the ramp, speaking to one of the humans. Trent stepped forward so he could see more of this world. Reaching the end of the ramp, he looked to the right. The white dock extended about half a mile further with ships of all sizes on either side. Beyond the dock was what seemed like an endless ocean. To the left, Trent could see the dock led to a pathway with gardens on either side as it wove its way to the only building. From where he stood he could make out even more creatures of all shapes and sizes walking around inside.

What the F-

"Trent, come on." Lexy's voice shook him from his thoughts.

Trent jogged to catch up with them. They walked at a quick pace up the dock and onto the path. Flowers of all colors and sizes pulled his attention. A sparkling navy blue bloom made him stop. The flower shimmered as he reached out to touch one of the teardrop shaped petals. His hand was slapped away.

"Don't touch," Lexy said, "unless you want an out of body experience."

She turned to catch up with Z who stood a few feet away.

Z shook his head. "Newbie."

Trent looked at the flower before stumbling to catch up.

"Wait, just touching it does that?"

Lexy kept her gaze forward. "That was a dream

walker plant. It's insanely powerful and some cultures use it to cause out of body experiences. Often times the "dream walker" as they are called, can communicate with spirits or even travel to another world or planes of existence."

Trent was shocked at how matter of fact she said this.

"They just let a plant like that grow on a busy path?"

They had reached the front of the building. Lexy stopped and faced Trent.

"This isn't Earth. Here, as on most enlightened planets, they don't kill plants just because it's an inconvenience. The plants and animals were here long before any beings, so they've all found a way to live together. Plants and animals respect our space and we respect theirs."

She turned and walked into the open first floor of the building. Trent didn't move, confused.

"You make it sound like plants have the ability to make decisions."

Beings all around him began staring at him, giving disapproving looks.

Lexy jogged back to him, grabbing his arm. She dropped her voice to a whisper.

"Do you want to draw attention to yourself? Many of these beings are plant in origin and they don't like it when others turn their nose up at them."

Still holding onto his arm she dragged him, with Z walking smugly behind, to the center of the building. Plants with large green leaves formed a crescent around four clear tubes that Trent guessed were elevators, because they were carrying beings to the upper levels and the unseen lower levels.

Lexy stopped in front of the third tube, "Do us all a favor and don't open your mouth. I have to find a way to explain how you managed to get onto MY ship unnoticed." They walked into a tube, "Ameran is going to kill me."

Lexy waved her hand in front of a small square to the left of the door and they began to move upward. Trent looked around, walkways led from the tubes to various levels. Beings mingled and disappeared through frosted doorways which reminded Trent of Earth's large office buildings. Some of the offices had no walls, some were clear, and some were frosted. As they passed one level he watched a room with frosted walls turn clear. He could see inside, as creatures gathered their papers from a table in what he could only guess was a conference room. Looking above them he saw sky and below was a clear floor. He began to wonder how this lift system worked since it didn't seem to have any parts to it beyond the floor and handrails.

Their ride was quiet and uncomfortable. Lexy was fidgeting and Z seemed to find the whole situation amusing. The tube stopped at the top floor. Lexy led the way out of the elevator, across the walkway and into an office. From the classic, elegant style, Trent guessed this was the Director's office.

Lexy's mind was racing. How could she explain away the presence of an Earthling?

Yes, director, I understand that allowing him to board my ship breaks the Illuminated's Code of Secrecy.

Yes, Director, I understand that I could lose my Stars for this.

Yes, I understand I could lose my ship.

I'm fucked.

Z walked past Lexy, throwing himself on a plush chair that was perfectly positioned in front of the black desk. Lexy ignored him as he propped his feet on the table. She looked around for Trent and cleared her throat to get his attention. He seemed to be lost in thought; frozen in the doorway. The director had a very impressive collection of ancient artifacts from various planets scattered around her office. A window looking out over the capital city took up an entire wall. The wall behind the desk was covered in constellations and small symbols indicating agency owned ships and their flight paths.

Since the Khunda belonged to Lexy, she knew that, if needed, their tracking beacon could be turned off, which they only did when they had mishaps or run-ins with mercenaries. Lexy and Z always managed to get their cargo to its destination in one piece, even if the Khunda and its crew acquired a few bumps and bruises along the way. So Ameran typically looked the other way. This, however, was different.

"Trent, can you sit here and not say a word when the director comes in?"

Lexy pointed to the other chair in front of the desk.

"If she talks to you, keep your answers short and refer to her as Director and-"

"Lex, chill," Z interrupted, "Golden child, remember?"

Trent sat down, his eyes searching the map for familiar constellations.

From behind them, Lexy heard the whooshing of the tubes and the soft fall of practical shoes on the glossy white floors. She put on her best smile and turned to face the approaching steps.

"Director I can-"

The director put up her hand stopping Lexy short. "Is this the Earthling?"

"Yes," Lexy choked out.

The director came to a stop in front of Trent, arms crossed.

"How did you get onto the Khunda?" she asked.

Trent's mouth opened but no sound came out. His

hands were clasped in his lap; his eyes were taking in Director Ameran. She had long legs, black hair and navy skin. The Director came from a world where human and plant genetics were combined. The experiments were part of an ancient genetic study banned hundreds of years ago. Her light pink blouse was tucked into a pencil skirt that showed off a slight curve.

"Did you follow Lexy? Or did you just happen upon the ship?" she asked.

"I, um-", Trent looked from Lexy to Ameran.

Lexy stepped forward. "Ma'am, if I may-"

Ameran's hand shot up again, silencing Lexy.

The director sat on the end of her desk, sighing.

"Trent- it is Trent?" She looked him in the eyes, smiling her political smile. Lexy knew she was working an angle.

"Trent, I must say, most Earthlings are easily frightened. Very few go toward a ship, let alone step on board."

She smiled.

Lexy noticed Ameran was looking at his uniform. Lexy pushed Z's elbow aside and sat on the arm of his chair.

"I thought Lexy was in trouble," Trent replied.

Trent's eyes never left Ameran's.

"You are brave Trent, but do you see my dilemma? You now know far more than the Illuminated has allowed for your planet. The royals have gone to great lengths to discredit and cover up any proof on your planet that we exist. What will stop you from talking if we allow you to return to Earth?" she asked.

That seemed to snap him out of it.

"What do you mean; allow me? You can't keep me here!" he snapped.

Lexy raised a finger. "Ah, actually they can. Top governments on Earth have been a part of the coverup and have an agreement with the Illuminated and the Royals that allows them to."

Trent stood, putting him face to face with the director. A smile spread across her face.

"I did what I had to in order to protect-" he started.

Lexy stood, putting her hand on his arm, stopping him.

"Trent just means that he promises not to say anything about this to anyone on Earth. Right? And that if you allow him to return home he could serve as - uh - a way to deter any possible sightings down the road," Lexy said in a calm voice.

Z snorted behind her. Lexy shot him a look at which Z began to flip through a folder he found on the corner of the desk.

The director stood, adjusting her blouse.

"You are former military, are you not?"

Trent nodded.

"Good. We need extra security for this job and, in return, we will allow you to go back to Earth. I have already appraised your uncle of the situation and he is taking care of Trent's disappearing act on Earth."

She walked around the desk and sat in her chair, leaving them all speechless.

Lexy shook her head. "Director, did I hear you correctly? Security? Surely you don't mean him," Lexy said, pointing at Trent.

"I do. You know as much as I do that good security is hard to come by, and he seems to have a need to protect. Maybe he can help keep you out of trouble. This might be the perfect way to keep an unenlightened stowaway out of the news scans."

She sat back, calm and relaxed.

Z's feet had slipped off the desk in shock. He allowed the folder to fall to the floor.

"Are you sure that's a good idea, Director?" he asked.

The director looked at Z, then at the papers on the floor. Z followed her gaze, then hastily picked up the papers and placed them back on the desk.

"Now I know you may want to talk about this a little more, but as you can see, I currently have twenty-two ships on missions and several more docking for missions pertaining to yours, which, by the way, is the transport of the newly chosen King of the Alpha Virgo."

Lexy's eyes shot open at the new information.

"A king? You want us to transport a king?"

"No. I don't want you to. You ARE transporting a king," Ameran corrected.

"Now, I have to get back to work. Lexy, you and Z will both get Trent here up to speed? Your packets have been sent to your ComBoards, and the Khunda is, as we speak, getting some much needed upgrades befitting your cargo."

She waved them off.

Lexy couldn't find a thought to hold onto. The idea that they had been chosen to transport a king was beyond words. Arms crossed, she turned with Z and Trent in tow.

"Oh, and Lexy, get him a uniform first. We don't want anyone seeing him in that."

Lexy nodded an acknowledgement.

The three of them walked back to the tubes, stepping aside to allow a group of grays to pass. They were silent as they all entered the tube and turned to see Ameran welcoming her next appointment with a perfect smile.

Trent crossed his arms. "What's wrong with my uniform?"

Khunda

Chapter Eight

The tube system took them past the main floor to a lower level. The door opened and Trent stepped forward, only to be stopped by Lexy's arm.

"Nope. This is Z's stop."

Z walked out, turned around, flipping off Trent as he moon-walked down the hall and into a room to the left.

"Are all of them like that?" Trent asked, scratching his head.

Lexy smirked, "Pretty much," she said, resting her head against the wall of the tube.

They stood in silence as the tube hummed into motion. Lexy turned to look at Trent who had the face of a man about to lose it. Lexy moved to stand in front of him.

"The first thing you are going to have to learn is don't take anything Z says seriously. He does things just to get a rise out of people. Second, you are about to find out that the universe is much bigger than Earthlings think, and even against all better judgement, you're still here. I have no idea what Ameran was thinking, but she knows best, I guess. Point is … breathe … just breathe," she said, smiling.

The tube stopped and Lexy walked out. Trent shifted into motion, jogging to catch up with her.

"Why do you call the director, Ameran?" he asked, looping his thumbs in his duty belt.

"She kind of became my outer-space-godmother after my parents died. She helped me get into the academy and she had the Khunda built for me. She knew my parents were saving up to build their own ship," Lexy replied, keeping her eyes forward.

"That's pretty awesome," Trent said, looking into the rooms as they passed.

Each room contained equipment Trent had never seen before as well as different species similar to Earthling tech geeks. Some were playing games on holo screens while others fiddled with parts. In one room he spotted a poster of a green creature with four arms, a large backside which was stuck out in a way to suggest it was an alien version of a pin-up. Trent shook the image from his memory.

Lexy led Trent into a large, plain room at the end of the hall. The walls, floor and ceiling were all made from the same blue metal. Trent crossed over the threshold and the door slid closed behind him.

"Stand like this," Lexy instructed as she held her arms out to her sides, looking over her shoulder at him. "They have to scan us before we can go in." She faced forward and Trent did as he was told.

A green beam of light coming from the wall in front of them passed over their heads and slowly moved to their feet. Red lights began flashing in each corner.

"Agh, I forgot," Lexy said, dropping her arms as she faced him. "Take off your belt and any other weapon you have on you."

"What? No, I'm not going to disarm on an alien planet. How do I know you aren't going to probe me?" Trent snapped.

"Why does everyone think that? Look, past this door is the supply room. No weapons allowed, no matter how primitive they may be," Lexy replied.

"Primitive? What is that supposed to mean?"

"The royal planets are more advanced then, what is that a Glock 21? 45 Cal? That's cute. Draw your gun," Lexy commanded.

"What?"

"Draw. Your. Gun." She repeated.

"No. Why? So a laser can come out of nowhere and fry me? Hell no!" Trent said, throwing his hands in the air.

"Lasers are obsolete," she said, crossing her arms. "Trust me, nothing is going to hurt you," she said, trying to hide a smirk.

Trent hesitated, not sure what to do, but he reached anyway. His arm stopped just above the gun's grip. He couldn't reach any further. He wasn't able to move anything but his face.

"Ah, Lexy. What the hell?"

"See, primitive. Basically, if any life form tries to draw a weapon or harm another, or let's say vandalize a statue, there are paralyzing protocols put into place. It's new technology we implemented a year ago. You may have a gun, but you can't use it."

Lexy gave him a smug look.

"So, would you like to place your weapons in the drawer?"

A drawer to his right slid open.

"Fine."

He could move again, so he removed his duty belt and placed it in the drawer, watching as it closed once he was done. Lexy was facing the front with her arms raised once more. Trent followed her lead and the scan began again. This time the corners of the room flashed green and the wall in front of them slid open.

A being identical to Z

"O.K., which of you is here for the anal probe?"

he asked, revving the power tool.

Trent took a step back.

"He's joking," Lexy said, giving the being a high-five as she passed him.

"Or am I?" the alien said, revving the drill.

"Lo, stop scaring my new security officer and log-in so I can get his gear," Lexy said.

She walked up to a long desk at the far side of what looked like a doctor's office waiting room. A neutral toned couch sat against the wall to the left, and calming images were spaced out along the walls. Lo looked deflated as he set the drill down on the floor and returned to the desk, typing on the glass surface.

"So Lex, when are you going to take me out on a date?" he asked.

She was flipping through symbols on the glass table top.

"Oh, I don't know, how many wives do you have now?" she responded with a laugh.

"You know that doesn't matter on my planet," he said with a shrug.

"But it does on mine…sometimes," she said.

Trent's curiosity was piqued as he stepped over the drill and walked up to the table.

"How many wives do you have?" Trent asked.

Lo and Lexy looked at him in surprise.

"Lex, my beauty, you finally found an Earthling that can hang. Twenty-three," Lo answered flatly.

"What? Wives? You have twenty-three wives?" Trent choked.

"I know, such a low number, but what can I say? I wait until I find true love before I marry someone."

He winked at Lexy who clearly had lost interest in the conversation and went back to flipping through symbols.

"What is that like?" Trent asked, scratching his chin. It was hard enough for him to imagine a house full of female grays chatting and baking.

"Way too much talking and yelling, that's why I found a job off planet," Lo replied. "But the love making-"

"Whoa," Lexy threw her hands over her ears, "Lo! No one, especially me, wants to hear that. Now both of you shut up and help me find the Royal Security gear," she snapped.

"Royal Security. Are you transporting a Royal?" Lo asked, his eyes somehow grew bigger.

"Apparently," Lexy mumbled.

"That's right, a Royal did die recently. The testing must be done," Lo said, returning to his typing.

Trent's eyebrows pinched together.

"Royals? Testing? What am I not understanding?"

"You catch the Earthling up and I'll find the

gear," Lo said, walking into the room behind the desk that was filled with rows of metal boxes and equipment.

Lexy, still leaning on the desk, turned to face Trent.

"The political system out here is more of a monarchy except they are educated since birth. Children of Royal families are taken away from their planets, their families, and everything in order to make them into leaders who make choices for the greater good. They are taught about the Ancients; which are the original species that brought together the first planets and civilizations, philosophy, religion, cultures, and laws. They rule for life. When one dies, those of age go into testing to see who is fit to rule that planet," Lexy explained.

"So one died and now we are transporting the new one to his planet?" Trent asked.

"That is what I have been told. This is a big deal, and Z and I hit a few bumps in the road on our last few drops so we really need this to go smoothly," she added, her eyes locked on the desk.

Trent could tell she was thinking about something because she was staring at the same symbols for a good minute before his voice shook her out of it.

"Define bumps," he said.

Lexy smiled, "You can ask Z that one."

"I think I'll keep it to myself then," Trent

laughed.

The muscles in his shoulders relaxed.

I didn't even know I was tense.

Lo returned, behind him a metal box scraped against the floor as he hauled it into the waiting room.

"Anyone wanna help? I am literally half your size," Lo grunted between breaths.

Trent hurried around the desk and took the box from him, setting it on the lower table behind Lexy. He noticed it didn't have any locks or latches, at least that he could see.

"Outta the way Earthling," Lo said, pushing past him and placing his hand on the lid. A click came from inside the box; Lo took the lid off and set it next to the box. Trent leaned over to look inside when Lo began removing the contents.

"One Alpha grade gun, a gun belt with leg holster, a pair of standard boots for Earthlings, a pair of black pants and a black top with CTA logo."

Lo turned to Trent, "Let me guess. You're a one-size-too-small-shirt kind of guy?"

"Funny. Do I need to try these on?" Trent asked, holding up the shoes and clothes.

"Nope, when we scanned you the system got all of you measurements," Lo explained.

"Alright boys, we need to get moving. Trent,

change into this stuff and put your uniform back in the box. Lo will send it to your quarters on the ship. We have more to do here," Lexy said, waving him toward a frosted door opposite the table.

Trent walked into what turned out to be a small dressing room, but before closing the door, he remembered something.

"What will happen to my gun?"

"I'll put it in the box," Lexy answered.

"Thanks."

He closed the door.

The new uniform was a perfect fit. The shirt allowed movement, while showing off his muscular arms. When he finished changing he walked out of the small room to the box which now held his police gear. He tucked his uniform next to his duty belt. His new gun was sitting on the table. Picking it up and sliding it into his leg holster, he turned to Lexy and Lo.

"How does this work?"

Lo's face told Trent that he had asked a stupid Earthling question.

"I'll go get you a ComBoard. Lexy has your ConnectBand."

Lo groaned, disappearing into the back room again.

Lexy was leaning on the table, typing away.

There was a band sitting next to her lighting up with different symbols and colors.

" It works just like your gun. Point and shoot. This is your new ConnectBand, which connects you to the Khunda as well as her entire crew. I am going to put this on your non dominant wrist and you are going to type in a pass code which is the only way to remove it. You can use any combination of characters and numbers," she said.

Trent looked at the screen, confused, because the symbols were alien to him.

Lexy cocked her head to one side, "Stand here and look at the screen," she ordered, stepping back so he could take her place.

Trent did as he was told. As he stood in front of the screen the weird symbols changed to English. *Cool*.

Lexy grabbed his arm and wrapped the band around his wrist. The ends clicked together like magnets.

"Now, put in your pass code and make sure you can remember it," she told him.

Trent thought about it for a second and then entered a code.

"Go ahead and say hello to the Khunda," she said, motioning to the band.

Trent awkwardly raised his wrist in front of his mouth and said, "Hello Khunda."

"Hello Officer Ryan Trent," the Khunda's gentle

voice responded, "How may I help you?"

"I am just testing out my new ConnectBand, Khunda."

"Congratulations Officer Trent, on your new ConnectBand. If you have any questions or requests, please feel free to ask. I am here to assist," she replied.

"Thank you, Khunda," his arm dropped back down to his side. "She is very polite," he noted out loud.

Lexy had returned to typing.

"If I have anything to do with it she'll stay that way. If I can get Z to stop teaching her new words" Lexy said, tapping the screen a little harder as she spoke.

"Teaching? Can she learn?" Trent asked.

"Yes, Khunda is a Bio Intelligent Dual Core Class A transport ship, which means she has a living neurological framework integrated into the core of the ship," Lexy answered in a matter-of-fact tone of voice.

"You mean there is a brain at the core of the ship." Trent's voice was calm, but this new information about the ship was making his head spin.

Lexy thought about it, her face pinching. "In a very basic way, yes," she answered.

She picked up a small device the size of a freckle.

"I am going to place this behind your ear so that if we meet any beings that speak another language it will translate for you through neural-connections."

She moved to his side and balanced on her tip-toes while placing the device behind his ear. As soon as it touched Trent's skin he felt a small pinch,

"That is the device attaching to your skin," she said. "You can do everything you normally do with it. If you want it removed there will be a button on your ComBoard to disengage it," Lexy explained.

Before Trent could ask any more questions, Lo returned with what looked like a tablet made entirely of glass except for a thin black line on the left edge. Lo handed it to Lexy who sat it on the table just above where she was typing. The tablet's handle lit up and strange symbols began to fill the screen.

Trent reached for it, wanting to make sense of the characters. But before he could touch it, Lexy slapped his hand away.

"No," she scolded.

Lo snickered.

Lexy sighed. "I am loading the ComBoard with all the information you may need, including our orders. This much data transfers through contact, so please leave it alone for a sec," she said.

Trent nodded. His eyes fell on Lo, who was typing on his side of the table. In the silence that followed Lexy's remark, he looked closer. Lo stood with his weight on one leg the other was bent lazily. He wore black boots, tactical pants and a dark green pullover with the agency logo on the chest. He had large, almond shaped eyes and his skull was elongated just like Z's. As Lo turned his head, Trent could see markings on his shoulders and the back of his neck.

Are those tattoos? Trent squinted, trying to get a better look.

"Look any harder and I'm going to take it the wrong way," Lo spit out.

Lexy looked at Trent, who froze where he was.

"Sorry, just curious," Trent said, rubbing his bicep.

Lexy looked at Lo in an apologetic way. "It's almost done loading. Is that all we need?" she asked Lo.

Lo pulled at his collar, hiding his markings. "I think so," he said. "They're loading the Wonder now, your girl is next," he said.

"Shit, that bag of hot air is here?" she asked.

The ComBoard flashed.

Lexy picked it up and tapped the screen. Satisfied, she handed it to Trent who was confused by Lexy's change in tone.

"What's the Wonder?" Trent asked.

Lexy sighed.

"It's another transport ship and it's Captain is a bit of an arrogant ass," she explained.

Walking to the box, Lexy closed it and pushed it against the wall. Lo typed something on the table and the wall behind the box opened and the box disappeared into the hole.

I have a lot to learn, Trent thought.

Lexy walked back to Lo and gave him a one-armed hug, kissing him on the head, "I'll see you when we get back. Tell your wives I said hey," she called over her shoulder and walked to the wall they came in through, which opened as she got closer.

"Will do Lex," he nodded at Trent. "You keep her safe or I will find a use for that drill." He chuckled.

Trent nodded, not quite sure if he was joking. He followed Lexy into the scanning room. This time they walked through without being scanned. Lexy was silent as they walked back to the tube system. Trent could tell she was tense, but didn't want to ask why for fear she would take it out on him. As the tube moved them back toward the surface, he decided to look at the ComBoard in his hands. The screen was in English and reminded him of his phone, which he had left in his patrol car. It had icons for each of its functions. The symbol on the top left of the screen was a Caduceus, the symbol used in the medical field on Earth. Curious, Trent tapped it. The screen filled with basic vitals and a real time ECG at the bottom.

"Wait, are these my vitals?" he asked, tilting the

screen so Lexy could see.

"Yes." She said flatly.

"How-" Trent was confused. These stats were very in depth; blood pressure, O2 saturation, heart rate, respirations, blood sugar and more.

"Your ConnectBand. It monitors your biological functions. Don't mess with it too much; you'll have a crash course in both the band and the board. I don't want you messing something up," she said, smiling at him.

Lexy reached over, swiping the screen with her finger which closed the app.

This is better than Star Trek, he thought.

Khunda

Chapter Nine

The tube stopped in the lobby. Lexy led the way out, turning to the right. The walkway they were on was lined with plants of varying heights and colors. This time Trent walked down the middle of the path, refusing to get too close to any of the plant life. They walked through a glass doorway into what looked like a cafeteria. Beings of all shapes, sizes and colors sat in front of plates filled with food Trent had never seen before. Lexy stopped in front of one of the screens with cycling pictures of foods, most of which Trent had never seen before. Lexy grabbed Trent's wrist and waved his band in front of a red light at the bottom. The pictures disappeared and were replaced with images of Trent's favorite breakfast foods.

Lexy must have known a question was coming because she answered before he could open his mouth.

"I identified you as an American Earthling and the band can read your nutrient levels so it came up with these as possible food choices," she explained. Her mouth twitched a little, as if she was trying to hold back a smile.

"Weird, but cool," Trent said, swiping through the food choices. He chose a plate of scrambled eggs, toast, a side of fruit and a large coffee.

Lexy stepped up to the screen next to his, swiped her band and made her choice.

"All those choices and you picked something healthy, Lex," Z said. "How am I going to survive this trip?" Z asked, walking up to stand beside Trent. "Move, my turn, I'm starving." He waved his hand at Trent, who stepped out of the way.

"We'll get a table," Lexy said as Z searched for his food.

Trent followed Lexy to a table in the corner. She dropped down into a chair facing the doors and said, "After we eat you will have a physical with the medical staff and then we'll have lunch on Khunda so I can give you the full tour then. This afternoon you'll have a crash course on protocol, the ConnectBand and ComBoard, and your basic duties. A program was loaded onto your ComBoard that can answer any questions and help you along the way," she explained.

"Ok," Trent looked around, "I can't believe this is

happening. I have been trying to just go with it, but last night I didn't believe in this stuff," he waved his hand toward the large room of different species, "and now I will be working security for an alien transport." He looked around the room again.

Lexy let his words sink in. She was raised around this so nothing about it seemed abnormal to her. She was struggling to understand what Trent was going through. She started picking at her nails.

Z sat down next to Lexy. "Why are we being quiet?" he asked.

"Trent's adjusting," she replied.

Trent looked at Lexy, not sure how she meant that.

Z leaned back, lacing his hands behind his head.

"Ah, it happens. You're handling it better than most. Lex, remember the last planet that became enlightened? They brought the leaders here to meet with leaders of enlightened planets in their constellation. One insulted the head of security and one puked in the main fountain and contaminated it." Z laughed.

"Aqua based species use the underground fountain systems to get around," Lexy explained.

Z went on, "And another slept with their pilot's daughter. That was fun to watch."

Trent skewed his face at Z.

"Not them sleeping together, the fight after her father found out. Gross. The pilot confronted him in the main park and proceeded to kick his ass," he explained.

"Some of us tried to break it up," Lexy scoffed.

"When a Lycan and a gypsy breed are fighting it out, what am I going to do?" Z dropped his arms, looking around.

Lexy went on, "Point being, you're taking this well, and if you have any questions, DON'T ask Z," she said pointedly.

Trent chuckled as their food arrived in a robot as tall as the table. It maneuvered through the maze of beings, approaching the table with lights flashing around its middle. Stopping next to them, its top slid open. A tray with toast, beans, over-easy eggs and a side of fruit came to the top.

"That's mine," Lexy said, grabbing the tray.

The next tray to appear was Trent's, and the last one had a large cup of what looked like a mud smoothie. Z took the cup, licking his lips. As he began drinking it, Trent stared at him, not sure if he should be impressed or grossed out. Z finished the whole cup in one go. Wiping his lips with the back of his hand, he belched and the stench of spoiled milk and fish guts wafted across the table.

"Ah, Z. What the hell?" Lexy threw her napkin at him, laughing.

Trent smiled and dug into his food.

Chapter Ten

After breakfast they walked to the medical floor. Z offered to stay with Trent, so Lexy left them bonding over crude jokes and war stories.

Boys.

Lexy walked toward the tubes, barely noticing the blur of beings passing her. As she reached the tubes she heard someone call her name.

"Captain Greggs! Wait. Please wait."

Lexy stopped, turning to see a short red haired man weaving through the crowd. He was a hobbit breed. It still amazed Lexy to what degree Earth's fairy tales and history were laced with alien life, yet they still refused to see what was right in front of them.

The man bent in half, panting, when he caught up to her.

" I- have- a - message from - the director-, "

He held up a hand, sucking in gulps of air. A man from inside the tube cleared his throat. Lexy turned to see three Nordic beings with scowls on their faces. She looked at her foot, realizing she was half in the tube which was keeping it from moving forward.

"Oh, sorry."

She stepped to the side and the tube shot into motion. She thought she heard one of the men grumble, "Earthlings."

She shook her head, turning back to the hobbit who was now using the railing for support. Lexy put her hand on his back.

"Do you need me to get help or-"

"No, No - I am- fine. Thank you. That is a long jog from control. The director would like to see you in the green house," he said.

His breathing had returned to normal now.

Lexy's face reflected her shock. "You ran here from control?"

He adjusted his shirt. "Yes, the director wanted to catch you before you left the building," he said

"Well, back to my post."

He waved, turned and jogged back into the crowd.

Lexy took the next tube to the main floor and exited at the back of the building. Garden beds lined the walk way. Each filled with flowering and fruit bearing plants from each of the enlightened worlds. At the head of each bed was an information screen that told about each plant and which species could eat it. The path ahead of her ended at the doors of a large greenhouse covered with vines blooming with multicolored flowers. Lexy stopped at Earth's bed and plucked off an apple. The director had commissioned the gardens on the island when she took over the CTA. In her groundbreaking speech she said that the gardens should be there for the education of each species and as a free source of food for those who need it. She was criticized for her words by several of the royals. At that time many of the outer constellations were facing revolts due to scarce food sources.

Lexy bit into the apple, *Ameran showed them.*

She entered the greenhouse and was greeted by various faces. The three long, potting tables were lined with kids in aprons. In front of each of them were pots filled with soil.

Lexy forced down the chunks of apple in her mouth that weren't fully chewed yet.

"Oh, sorry. I didn't mean to interrupt," she said, tossing the rest of the apple into the compost box to her left.

"Not at all, Captain Greggs," Ameran said.

Standing at the other end of the table she smiled

at Lexy.

"Kids, this is Captain Lexy Greggs. She is one of my best transport Captains. She used to be an intergalactic gardening student when she was your age. As you can see, she now prefers to eat rather than garden," Ameran said, causing an outbreak of giggles from her students.

Lexy waved. "Hi, kids. Stay in school," even she knew how lame that sounded, "I'll just wait outside."

"Nonsense, Lexy. Help me up here," Ameran waved at a table against the wall. "As for the rest of you, please continue repotting the nova plants until they all have a new home."

All of the children continued their work as Lexy joined Ameran.

"How are your aunt and uncle?" she asked.

Lexy shrugged, "They're fine. Although, I'm guessing Greggs is freaking out trying to cover up Trent's disappearance."

Ameran handed her a pair of gloves.

"I assume you remember how to repot a nova plant?"

"Yes," Lexy answered, smirking at the question.

Pulling a pot from the shelf, she began scooping sandy soil into it.

Ameran did the same

"I am sure you are wondering why I gave you this

mission and why I went easy on your stowaway."

Lexy snorted, "Yeah. I'm curious, but I also trust that you have your reasons."

"I appointed you because this prince is the son of the Alpha Leo king," Ameran said in a hushed tone. Lexy knew what that meant. The king had executed a group of humanoids born and raised as security for the Royals. The group was accused of starting a battle that killed several guards. Many of the Royal constellations condemned the king's actions because he had their families killed, children and all.

"So you think Z and I are the better choice?" Lexy asked, stuffing a small, leafy plant into the pot.

Ameran's lips pulled at the corners. "You and Z have managed to get out of more troubling situations than I care to count. The point is, just as you trust me to make decisions, I trust you to handle the situation put in front of you. And as for your stowaway, we are going to need all the security we can get. I had his military history pulled and he is a great fighter. I only worry his new found enlightenment could cause some issues."

Lexy took off her gloves. "Honestly, I think he is handling it well. Maybe he's had an encounter before," Lexy laughed.

Ameran tucked a piece of hair behind Lexy's ear. "You so remind me of your mother. She was always joking on the outside while panicking on the inside." Both she and Lexy laughed.

Lexy set her gloves on the table. "Well, I have to get to work. See you when I get back."

"Of course," Ameran responded, squeezing Lexy's hand.

Lexy left as memories of her and Z throwing dirt at each other from across the greenhouse tables invaded her thoughts.

Chapter Eleven

There was more work being done to the ship than she had ever seen before. The typical mechanics were checking all of the ships systems, the supply rooms were being stocked with everything they would need, and designers were working in the rooms to ensure that the new Royal and his entourage would be comfortable. Lexy rolled her eyes as a storage box full of gold plates was loaded.

You have got to be kidding me.

She decided to hide on the bridge. Everything seemed to need her approval. She was stopped what seemed like every five feet to approve something. Finally, making it to the bridge, she quickly set to work loading star charts and alternate paths when a woman, too dressed up for Lexy's taste, entered the bridge with a flustered reptilian species in tow.

The woman was robust and had feathers instead of hair. She wore a purple dress that showed off her ankles, but dragged behind her as she walked. Her waist was pulled in by a black and gold corset. Lexy tried to look anywhere but at the woman's breasts that were trying to escape her dress.

"You cannot expect a member of the Royal family to sleep on that brick you call a bed. I need an approval for a feather based mattress at the very least," the woman demanded.

Lexy looked from the woman to the reptile behind her.

"Hello," she said, "I am Alexandrea Greggs, Captain of the Khunda." She extended her hand, but the woman just looked at it. "I am sure the director herself put in the spec orders down to every detail. I approve whatever the director has ordered."

The woman huffed. "I am sure you are used to transporting ordinary beings who would not object to this level of … comfort, but we are talking about the future King of an Alpha planet."

She crossed her arms and stared Lexy down.

"Do YOU think that a King of an Alpha planet should be subjected to sleeping on a bed that other beings have slept on?"

That pissed Lexy off. She stood, crossing her

arms, and stepped closer to the woman.

"Short answer: yes. Long answer: if you have a problem with it, go talk to the director. I have more important things to think about, like getting the future King from his blessing to his new home safely. So if you don't mind, get off my bridge," Lexy said, nodding at the door.

The woman's eyes shot open in shock, and then she turned and stomped out. Waves of fabric followed her. The reptilian, with a smile, extended his hand to Lexy.

"Captain, it's been a pleasure." He turned and walked out, stopping to nod at Trent and Z as they walked onto the bridge.

Z gave Lexy a questioning look, "What had her thong in a wad?"

"She was just pissed about beds," Lexy said, returning to their flight plans.

"I'm going to guess she hasn't been satisfied in one for a long time," Trent commented, setting his Com-Board on the navigation desk.

Lexy couldn't believe what she had just heard. "What?"

Z chuckled and returned to his typing. "He isn't that bad, Lex."

Lexy typed in her confirmation for the flight plans and then said to Trent, "Come on, I'll introduce you to Khunda."

Entering the elevator, Lexy pushed a symbol on the screen to the left of the doors. The top of the screen flashed red; she placed her hand on the flashing light.

"You have access to most of the ship, some sections are off limits to everyone except the captain, pilot and security," Lexy explained.

The light beneath her hand flashed green and the elevator began to move. She turned to face the back wall.

"This screen can show you a map of the ship, each section, and even where everyone is. Just wave your ConnectBand in front of one of the corners," she said, motioning for Trent to swipe his band. When he did, the screen changed from its normal moving galaxy image to full plans of the Khunda.

Lexy pointed to each level in turn. "Level 1 is the cargo bay, level 2 the ship's core and engineering, level 3 has extra quarters, you will be staying there with the rest of the staff, level 4 is guest quarters which will be all Royal attendants and the soon-to-be king, level 5 is the common space with kitchen, gym, medical rooms, and gazing room. Level 6 is the bridge with my, Z's and the head of security's quarters."

Trent nodded in acknowledgement. The door opened and they stepped out into the cargo bay. The bay doors were still open and workers of all types were loading supplies.

"You remember this," Lexy teased. "Storage is back there, jump ship is there," she said, pointing as she spoke, "Pretty self-explanatory."

She turned and walked back into the elevator. Trent followed. Lexy motioned for him to choose the floor. He looked at the panel in front of him and the symbols changed to English. Tapping *Level 2*, the elevator moved. When the doors opened they walked into a circular hall. Lexy led him to the left and entered a pass code into the panel next to the doors. Once the doors opened Trent took in the room. It was lit by a soft glow emanating from a thick glass tube that sat on a pedestal in the center of the room. Four blue lights ran under the clear floor from the pedestal to each corner of the room. When Trent looked down he could see thick wires under the transparent floor.

Lexy pointed to the tube on the pedestal, "This is Khunda's core. Her brain," she said, smiling.

Trent looked closer as a round mass pulsed with the soft blue light at chest height inside the glass and then stared, transfixed.

"It looks like a real brain."

"That's because it is," Lexy replied.

"Really?" Trent asked, looking closer.

"Yes, Khunda uses neurons from a biological donor. This allows her to learn and understand her living counterparts," Lexy explained as she began to walk around the core.

"That's gross, but kinda cool," Trent chuckled.

"Each of the four corners control a different part of the ship's systems."

Trent looked around the room. Lexy looked at him, studying his interest in the core. Trent was beginning to think she was waiting for him to lose his mind. Not many people could learn about the existence of one alien race without losing their mind, let alone the existence of so many. Trent met her eyes and smiled.

Lexy clasped her hands behind her back and led the way back to the elevator where Trent pressed the button for *Level 3*. The elevator moved and the doors open to an oval room with four doors spread around the walls. Tables were spaced around the center. Only a few people were working on this floor.

"These are the staff quarters. Girl's rooms are these doors, boys the other two. You will be in this one."

The door opened as they approached. Across the room from them the door to a group bathroom stood open. The bed closest to the bathroom had a metal box on the floor next to it.

"This is yours," Lexy pointed to the box.

Trent smiled. "This reminds me of the military."

"I hope in a good way."

"Always." He smiled.

Their eyes met and Lexy could tell that his memory was a good one.

"Let's go, we have more to do."

Lexy led the way this time, pressing the symbol for *Level 5*.

"What about level 4?" Trent asked.

"Agh, that diva you ran into is fluffing that level up for the Royal cargo. I really don't want to see what she's doing to my ship," Lexy responded, pinching the bridge of her nose.

"This is a big deal, huh?"

"Yeah." Lexy sighed.

"Well, I'll do my best not to embarrass you," he said, giving her an innocent smile.

"Ha! I work with Z. I'm used to embarrassed," she said, smiling at Trent's attempt at levity.

The doors opened to the common room that was alive with movement. Two grays were stocking the freezer behind the kitchen counter, another was putting the new table settings away and several other beings were wandering around making adjustments to the decor.

"Kitchen is on the left, gym and medical rooms are straight ahead, gazing room on the right. If, for any reason, our guests need to be 'secured', chairs come out of the walls of this room."

"Secured?" Trent sounded hesitant.

"Don't ask." Lexy waved away his question and walked into the kitchen.

"Let's see what we have for lunch. Oh look, prepackaged meals."

She tossed one to Trent. "Looks like the Earthlings got turkey sandwiches, an apple and almond butter. I can find you something different if you want," she offered. "They just know this is my favorite lunch."

"This looks good," Trent said.

"Let's take these upstairs. Z has to be starving by now and I can't stand to watch what they are doing to my ship," she said, picking up a large, sealed cup and thanking the chef that slid it in front of her.

Heading back to the bridge, Lexy poked her head in to tell Z lunch was in her room, he nodded in response. Trent followed her into her quarters. Lexy set her and Z's lunch on the coffee table in front of the couch and walked to the kitchen. She grabbed a jar out of the cabinet and began making a pot of coffee.

"What do you want to drink? I have water, apple juice, tea and coffee. I suggest coffee because the jet lag is going to start kicking in," Lexy called over her shoulder.

"Coffee it is," he replied.

Lexy filled two cups as Trent took the seat next to the couch and opened his lunch.

He was looking at Z's cup, while Lexy set their

coffee on the table.

"What does he eat?" Trent asked. "This looks worse than his breakfast," he said in disgust.

"Z's species doesn't normally eat solids. Most of the time they eat liquids because of their digestion. You don't want to know what they blend together for the grays," she explained, opening her lunch.

"No, I don't," Trent mumbled, taking a bite of his sandwich.

There was a knock on the door.

"Come in Z," Lexy called out, taking a sip of her coffee.

Z walked in, pushing past Lexy to sit in the middle of the couch. He rubbed his hands together and said, "Lunch time!"

"Sit anywhere you want," Lexy scoffed.

Z didn't respond; he was busy opening his lunch. He shook the bottle then peeled back the seal and began to chug.

"So, do you have any questions, Trent?" Lexy asked before taking a bite of her sandwich.

"Actually, yeah, how did you get into all of this? I mean you're from Earth, right? If we aren't 'enlightened' then how did you get this job?" he asked.

Z wiped his mouth with the back of his hand and looked at Lexy.

Shrugging, she responded, "Earth isn't an enlightened planet, but it is a visited planet-"

"Are you kidding me?" Z said, leaning back on the couch with his hands behind his head. "We created your planet. We are crawling all over it like ants."

Lexy dropped her head into her hands.

"I was going to leave that for another time, but since you decided to chime in. Yes, a group of grays created Earth," she snapped.

Trent choked on his sandwich. "What do you mean, created?"

"Before Earth was habitable the grays needed a planet to grow their genetic test subjects. They started with creatures they found on other planets and mutated them from there. The science was to find a way to save their species from extinction. At the time, they were involved in The Great War in the Crux constellation. The war went on for centuries and killed most of their kind. So once they perfected the science, they wiped the planet and started again. They were trying to make a species they could transplant their consciousness into," Lexy explained.

Trent took a long sip of coffee, staring at the bottom of his cup.

"You mean they created and then wiped out the dinosaurs?"

"Yeah, then we began to create your species,

which were also used as workers in space and we created two other planets using the DNA. "

Z stood, squeezing past Lexy to toss his bottle in the trash. "I've got work to do."

He shot them the peace sign on his way out.

Trent looked at Lexy questioningly.

"Some of the grays believe Earth should be free and some believe genetic testing should keep going for the possibilities. The science has been tied up in the Royal courts since the Greeks. The grays have gotten a lot of prejudicial backlash because of it. Z doesn't like talking about it." Lexy tore off her crust.

"So, a group of aliens could own the Earth and the people living there don't know about any of it?" Trent asked.

"Pretty much. The Earthlings who live and work in space have been working toward enlightenment consideration. The committee thinks Earth won't handle it well," Lexy responded, "As for how I got started, my mother was of Royal blood, she was born in the Virgo Constellation. After she aged out of the testing to become a queen she decided to join the Intergalactic Flight Academy. Where she met my father who was studying to be a captain. His side of the family has been in the know for centuries. He was one of the first Earthings to be allowed into the academy. I was raised both on Earth and in space.

They ate the rest of their lunch in silence. Lexy watched as Trent wrinkled his forehead, most likely processing this new information. They both knew that if this information ever went public, society on Earth would self-destruct. She had read about several planets that reacted negatively to their enlightenment. Some of them had survived, but others were now wasteland planets. She was torn over enlightenment for Earth. On one hand, she knew Earth should be liberated and free from genetic testing, but she also didn't trust humans to react in a logical way. No matter which way the committee ruled, her home planet would never be the same again.

Chapter Twelve

After lunch, they went to the gazing room to meet the head of security, Apaleo. Lexy had worked several missions with him and knew he could be an ass, but she respected him because he always got the job done. Trent was looking out the window at the dock and the ship parked next to them.

"If you want to, you can ask Khunda and she will show you what you want," Lexy said.

"For example; Khunda, show me the Milky Way Galaxy on the hologram."

A burst of light filled the room. Trent, who was standing in the center of the room, was now standing in the middle of the Galaxy.

"Cool," he said, looking around.

Lexy walked toward Trent.

"Khunda, can you show me Earth?" she asked.

The two stood in the center of the moving holo-gram as Earth was highlighted in the swirling mass.

"Enlarge,"

She grabbed Trent's arm as the planet grew in front of them. Trent let her direct his hand to the side of their planet and move it slightly to the right, making Earth spin. They both laughed at the sight. The door slid open and Lexy dropped his hand, as a tall, older man with short dark hair, tan skin and a square jaw walked in.

He nodded at Lexy. "Captain, it's a pleasure to be working with you again."

"Hello, it's good to have you onboard. Trent, this is Apaleo, head of Security for this mission."

Trent extended his hand, but Apaleo just glared at it.

"Apaleo, this is Officer Trent, from Earth. The director hired him for this mission," Lexy explained.

Apaleo crossed his arms. "The director told me about the situation. This won't be a free ride, Earthling. You will stay by my side at all times, do exactly as I say, and don't talk to anyone. As soon as you are done with your crash course, come find me."

He turned and walked out.

Trent faced Lexy. "Well, he seems nice."

Lexy shrugged, "That's Apaleo for you. He called

you Earthling, so I guess he doesn't hate you."

"Yeah, about that, why did he call me Earthling? Isn't he…" Trent trailed off.

Lexy snapped her fingers and the lights came back on.

"He is an altered breed from one of the other planets they created with various combinations of the DNA they got from us. His breed was created to be protectors, strong and cunning. They're used in the guard and to protect the Royals."

Trent sighed, "Okay, so who is taking me on this crash course?" he asked, leaning against the railing.

"One of our techs, I think they are sending over Ali. She's cool, but be careful. She is a reader, which means she can read your mind if you're not careful."

Lexy put her elbows on the railing, positioning herself the appropriate distance from him to keep the atmosphere casual.

"Alright, I've come to the conclusion that I am going to accept everything you say and if I have any questions I will ask you in private so that I don't seem lost all of the time," Trent told her.

Lexy laughed, "Deal."

The door slid open, a woman with blonde hair and piercing green eyes walked in. Her hair was pulled into a ponytail, showing her pointed ears. She stood almost as tall as Trent, her thin frame reminding him of a Tolkien elf.

This must be the tech geek, Ali, Trent thought, pushing himself off the railing.

Lexy was already up and hugging Ali.

"I'm glad you're back, Ali. How was the training?"

Ali smiled, "Great, we got to meet a lot of the leaders, they were very welcoming. We got a lot done, but we are going back next month to help with some of the glitches we found.

Lexy seemed to understand what Ali was talking about, but Trent felt out of the loop again, which he was starting to get used to. He shifted his weight to his right leg.

"I'd say it sounds fun, but it doesn't," Lexy said, smiling. "Ali, this is Officer Trent. He is a new member of this mission and is in need of a crash course."

Ali extended her hand to Trent, "Trent, it's nice to meet you. So…How "crash course" are we talking?" she asked as Trent shook her hand.

"I just found out about aliens and space travel a few hours ago so I would say very crash course, he answered.

Ali's eyes shot open. "No shit. Well, we have our work cut out for us. Let's get started." Ali walked to the screen on the wall and began pushing buttons.

"I'm going to leave you to it," Lexy said.

She gave them a small wave as the door slid closed behind her. A blue being that came

up to Lexy's hips approached her.

"Captain, can we get you to sign off on a delivery?" he asked.

"Yes, lead the way," Lexy replied, wishing she could stay hidden on the bridge all day.

The afternoon had gone by in a blur. Lexy had been pulled this way and that, asked to approve everything that was brought onboard, as well as the itinerary and menus. By evening, her brain was throbbing and her feet had mysteriously grown two sizes since lunch. Slinging herself on her couch and covering her face with a pillow, she contemplated napping before dinner. Her door slid open and she figured it was Z coming in based on the quiet footsteps coming towards her. She heard him flop into the chair at her feet.

"A Royal transport is way too much work," he said.

Lexy took the pillow off her face, "I agree."

Someone knocked. "Who is it?"

"It's Officer Trent, Captain," Khunda answered.

"Come in," the door slid open and Trent walked in looking freshly showered.

"You had time to shower? Lucky," Z stretched and stood looking at Lexy. "Are you ready to face the troops, Lex?"

"Might as well. How do I look?" she asked, standing.

"Like a human," he said and walked out.

"Ass," Lexy called after him.

"The troops?" Trent asked Lexy.

"We eat dinner with the whole crew inside the CTA the night before departure, which includes you so let's go," she said, pushing him out the door.

They joined Z in the elevators.

"How was your day, cowboy?" Z asked, crossing his arms as he leaned against the wall, clearly exhausted.

"That was about as fun as the first day of boot camp. Why did I have to run laps around the docks?" he asked.

Z shrugged, "I guess he wanted to sort out pecking order. You humanoids are weird."

This made Lexy snort. The doors opened to the cargo bay and they walked down the ramp and up the dock into the CTA lobby. Lexy stepped up to a screen next to the tube system and scanned her arm band. When she returned Trent and Z were exchanging war stories.

"Alright boys, time to put on our game faces."

Z snapped his feet together, "Yes, ma'am."

Lexy rolled her eyes and walked down a hallway behind the tubes, the boys followed, still sharing stories. They walked through a large sliding door into what looked like a boardroom. The far wall was lined with framed blueprints of various ships. In the center of the room a long table was set for a large group. The rest of the ten member security team sat along the far side, while two chefs, two maids, three stewards and three support staff of varying beings sat along the close side. Lexy took her spot at the head of the table with Z to her right and Apaleo on her left. Trent took his seat next to the Apaleo. Lexy was still standing as she addressed the crew.

"It is good to see all of you. I am your Captain, Alexandrea Greggs. This is your pilot, Zephla of Orion. Our mission is to escort the future King of the Virgo capital planet from his blessing to his seat on Alpha Virgo. This is a very important mission, and it will be highly publicized. I expect nothing but the best and hardest working crew. I know many of you, but some of you are new," she smiled at Trent. "We will complete our mission as a team. With that I hope you enjoy your dinner."

Lexy sat in her chair as the crew politely clapped. A line of waiters walked into the room, each carrying two trays, which they set in-front of their respective diners. The room filled with conversation. The tray set in front of Lexy held a 6 oz. steak, medium rare, mashed potatoes and asparagus. Trent's plate mirrored hers; this was the meal that was prepared for the Earthlings. The dinner passed with laughs, stories and discussions about the mission.

"I hope we get to watch the ceremony. I've never seen a Royal crowned."

"I heard they had a hard time with the testing this round."

"What if the rebellion tries to disrupt the ceremony?"

Apaleo cleared his throat at the comment that came from a younger security officer. "Watch your tongue," he said. "We do not want to create fear or gossip among the crew."

Lexy raised an eyebrow. "I agree with Apaleo, but I will add that my crew and cargo have nothing to worry about. We have the best security, the best pilot and Khunda is the best ship in the fleet."

The two maids giggled, catching Lexy's attention. Under her inquisitive stare one of the maids decided to explain herself.

"Sorry, Captain, but I worked on the Wonder for a few missions and I heard that she was the best ship."

Lexy's cheeks began to burn and she slid her hands under the table, twisting her cloth napkin.

"While the Wonder and her Captain are very capable, they were not chosen for this important mission."

Her tone silenced the giddy maids, who then turned their attention to Trent. The servers brought out a variety of colorful desserts and set them in the center of the table. Lexy caught Trent's eye.

"Stick with what looks familiar. You don't want to know what the others are made of," she said.

He nodded in understanding and reached for what looked like a chocolate eclair.

The dinner ended with a round of drinks and the crew returned to Khunda as an excited and tipsy group. Trent, Lexy and Z brought up the rear.

"So Trent, the ladies seem to like you." Z elbowed Trent's side "If you need a wingman…"

"This is why I would rather haul objects. I wouldn't have divas throwing glitter all over my ship and I wouldn't walk in on anyone doing the nasty in the storage room," Lexy huffed.

Z looked up at her with a knowing look, "Lex you have to …"

"Don't tell me what I have to do," Lexy snapped, walking ahead.

Trent watched as she disappeared into the group ahead of them.

"Did I miss something?"

Z sighed, "You tell her I told you and I will toss your ass into orbit. Got it?"

Trent nodded.

"She and another captain had a thing. Lexy fell hard for him, until she-"

"Found him in the storage room with someone else," Trent finished.

"Not just one someone, two. You should have seen that fight. I thought she was going to kick him out the cargo door on reentry. Kinda funny for me, I always thought he was a puffed up asshole."

"Was it the captain of the Wonder?"

"Yeah, how did you know?"

"I just noticed she reacted to the name when Lo said it."

"Agh, he may be a tech god, but he isn't good with emotions."

They walked up the ramp into the cargo bay. A few members of the crew were waiting for the elevator.

Z stopped just inside the doors. "Khunda, is the crew accounted for?"

"Yes, Z, all crew members are on board."

"Time to lock up for the night."

"Cargo door closing," Khunda said.

The door moaned as it lifted off of the dock and connected with the frame.

Z and Trent were in the elevator alone.

"You let me know if any of the crew gives you crap. I think they'll be more interested, but some of them look like they are straight out of training, so you never know."

"Thanks," Trent nodded at him.

Then the doors opened to the crew quarters and he stepped out into the busy common room. Z leaned his head back against the wall as the elevator shifted into motion.

Lexy was right, transporting objects was easier.

Khunda

Chapter Thirteen

The next morning Lexy rolled over as the lights turned on, the ship's version of an alarm clock. Slowly easing one eye open, her bedside table came in focus. It was already a mess, a notebook was sitting next to a water glass which was behind an empty candy wrapper and her laptop was sitting on the far edge. Still groggy, she rolled onto her back, rubbing the sleep from her eyes. Letting out a deep sigh she remembered she was aboard Khunda, and today was the first day of their Royal mission. Letting out a loud groan she flopped back over on her stomach and pulled a pillow over her head.

"Khunda," she said in a muffled voice.

"Yes, Captain?"

"Do you think anyone would notice if I went back to sleep?"

"Most of the crew is already awake, so I do believe they will notice your absence."

"Dammit," Lexy threw off her covers and sat up on the edge of the bed.

"Khunda, could you please read today's schedule to me?"

Khunda began reading off the long list of tasks that were set for the day.

Lexy stood, stretched and walked into the bathroom, turning the hot water on in the shower. She was fully awake by the time she finished her shower. She dressed and left her quarters, grabbing an apple from the fruit bowl on the coffee table. Stepping out onto the curved hallway, she looked over the banister to the common space below. The room was filled with crew members eating breakfast and chatting excitedly. This made Lexy smile. Even though she wasn't all that happy about sharing her ship with so many others, she did understand their excitement about being part of a Royal transport. It was rare that a member of the Royals came into power. It was even rarer to have a Royal crowned as the leader of an Alpha planet.

She took a bite of the apple and walked onto the bridge. It was empty. Taking the opportunity, she threw herself on her chair and propped her feet up on the console. She took a few more bites out of the apple before tossing the core into the waste bin, a small hole in the wall next to her.

"Khunda, can you open a comm to Z?"

"Yes, Captain. Communication is open."

"Z, where the hell are you?"

A loud moan came through the speakers.

"Z, get your ass out of bed."

A very muffled explicit ticked her off.

"Khunda, play N'Sync at full volume in the pilot's sleeping quarters, please."

"Yes, Captain"

Bye, Bye, Bye blared over the comms followed by a string of insults directed at Lexy.

"I'll see you in ten, Z."

Lexy touched a button on the console, turning off communications. She rested her forehead on her knees. The tension in her shoulders had eased slightly when Apaleo and Trent entered the bridge.

"Good morning, Captain. I hope you rested well."

"Yes, I did. Thank you," Lexy said, letting her feet drop to the floor.

"Did I just hear The Backstreet Boys coming from Z's room?" Trent was trying to hide his amusement.

"N'Sync, and yes, sometimes the only way to wake him up is to piss him off."

The door opened and Z dragged himself onto the bridge without saying a word. He slid into the pilot's chair while Trent pretended to be focused on his ComBoard. Lexy couldn't help but laugh at Z's disheveled appearance, but he was obviously not amused. Apaleo seemed confused by the whole situation.

"Officer Trent, come with me. We need to do final security checks before we take off. If that is alright with you, Captain?"

"Yes, whatever you need to do. Just let me know as soon as you're done so we can start the pre-flight checks."

Apaleo left with Trent following. Lexy began to recheck the flight plans. Her stomach was starting to twist. This flight would be a huge milestone in her career as well as her crew's. She was hoping it would go as planned.

They were set to take off just after lunch. Everyone rushed around the ship completing final checks. After checking and rechecking their flight plans, Lexy made her way down to the cargo bay to do an all systems check on the jump ship. The silence inside the small ship was a contrast to the rest of the ship that was teeming with personnel going about their duties. She always found the jump ship was the perfect place to hide whenever she needed to think through things. Letting herself relax into the chair, she closed her eyes and began taking deep breaths while visualizing the air filling her abdominal cavity before she pushed it all out. She learned this technique while transporting the Dalai Lama to his planet of origin. Smiling, she remembered how he followed her around like a puppy giving her advice at every turn. At the time it frustrated the hell out of her, but over the course of their trip they became friends. She often sent him messages asking for advice.

Letting out a long, slow breath, she opened her eyes, leaned over the console and tapped a button recording program. A hologram screen appeared in front of her. Half of it showed the face of the Dalai Lama and the other half showed her face.

"Hey. I hope this message finds you well. I saw on the news feed that you were somewhere in the Virgo constellation. I assume you're doing what you do well, pestering people. I know you're off doing amazing things helping others find inner peace and enlightenment." Lexy paused, not sure how much she should say. "I guess what I just wanted to say hi and see how you are doing."

Lexy heard the sound of boots walking up the jump ship's ramp, "I hope to hear from you soon, Namaste, old man."

Lexy quickly hit the button to turn off the communication recording. She turned around to face the owner of the boots. Trent stood there, one eyebrow raised. His grease covered arms made Lexy's pulse speed up.

"Can I help you?"

"Did you just send a message to the Dalai Lama?"

"You really need to NOT eavesdrop. It's rude."

She raised an eyebrow at him and turned her chair back to the console.

Trent stepped between her chair and the pilot's chair.

"I'm sorry. I didn't mean to listen in. Apaleo had me cleaning his weapons when I heard you talking. I just wanted to see how you're morning was going."

A small smile pulled at the edges her lips. Lexy cleared her throat.

"Well, that's very nice of you. My morning is going well. How about yours?"

"To be honest, I don't think Apaleo likes me that much. Not that I'm complaining. I just wasn't sure if that's normal. I'm starting to question my perception of normal."

"That's pretty normal for him. Anytime I'm his captain he's respectful, but outside of our missions he can be a straight up dick. But I kind of feel bad for him, he comes from a planet in the Leo constellation that was terraformed and created for the purpose of breeding warriors."

"What does that mean?"

"The whole planet of humanoids are born and raised for the sole purpose of protecting the Royals and fighting their wars."

"They don't have a choice?"

"Some have tried to rebel, some are still trying, but out here things are different. No one will hire a warrior for anything other than protection or fighting."

Silence fell as they reflected on the conversation.

Trent jumped when his ConnectBand vibrated.

"Crap. It's Apaleo. I guess I'll see you later."

He stood, shoving his hands into his pockets and, giving Lexy a shrug, walked down the ramp.

Lexy finished the checks for the jump ship and went back to the bridge. She found Z in a better mood and rocking out to Queen. Her stomach grumbled.

"Khunda, can you open up a comm to Apaleo?"

"Communication open, Captain"

"How are the security checks going?"

"Almost done, Captain. I should be finished in ten minutes."

"Okay, just let me know. Com off."

Z stood, stretching his arms over his head.

"Wanna grab some food?"

"Sure."

Even though her stomach was growling, every time she thought about the cargo she felt like throwing up, so she didn't actually feel very hungry. She and Z stepped out of the elevator and walked into the common room. The few crew members eating, stood.

Lexy held up her hand, "New rule: you don't stand when I enter the room."

"But Captain," a handsome steward started, looking nervous, "it's protocol."

"Yes it is…" Lexy stepped closer so she could read his name badge, "Hermes, but seeing how this is my ship, I would really appreciate it if you didn't. So please sit down and enjoy your lunch."

The room filled with hushed chatter as the crew took their seats.

Lexy walked to the kitchen counter and asked one of the chefs for almond butter toast and a large cup of green tea. Z placed his order and turned to stare at Lexy.

"What?"

"I think you scared the new guy."

"He'll live. What do you mean by new guy? They all look new. Which is odd, this is a very young crew for a Royal mission."

Z shrugged. "Apaleo did the background checks and picked the crew himself. He must see something we don't."

Lexy was about to comment but decided not to when the chef pushed a tray in front of her.

"Enjoy your meal, Captain."

"I will. Thank you."

She found a table away from the rest of the crew. The elevator doors opened and Apaleo walked in followed by Trent. Apaleo walked to the chef and ordered his lunch, while Trent stood just outside the elevator doors looking around the room. When he saw Lexy and Z he gave a small wave. Lexy nodded back. Trent ordered his lunch. Lexy and Z were talking about the flight plans when he walked up to the table.

"Mind if I sit with you?"

"I don't know newbie. I think you might have to answer a few questions first."

"Z, don't be a dick," Lexy scolded.

Lexy used her foot to push out the chair next to her. Trent set his tray on the table. Z threw his foot on top of the chair.

"Why is six afraid of seven?"

Lexy rolled her eyes.

"Because seven eight nine."

Trent slapped z's foot off the chair and sat down.

"Am I the only one in this universe that didn't know that joke?"

"Yes," Lexy and Trent said.

Z shook his head in disbelief and then turned to Trent.

"How was your morning?"

"Well, I didn't start my day jamming out to N'-sync, but so far so good."

Z glared at Lexy. "Karma is a bitch, and so is our Captain."

"Don't get mad at me. You were late this morning," Lexy said, picking at her toast.

"Do you understand that I've had that damn song stuck in my head all day?" Z grumbled.

Trent laughed.

Lexy had finished her tea, but her toast sat in front of her half eaten.

"If you'll excuse me boys, I'm going to start flight checks."

Z sighed and chugged the rest of his lunch.

"Wait for me Lex. See you on the bridge newbie."

Lexy placed her plate and tea cup on the kitchen counter. Preflight checks would take about an hour, meaning they would leave on time.

So far so good.

They were about halfway through checks when Apaleo and Trent entered the bridge. Trent turned to sit in the navigation chair behind Z, but Apaleo stopped him by placing his hand on his shoulder.

"You can take a seat over there," he waved his hand in the direction of one of the chairs behind Lexy, who is still hunched over the console triple checking their flight plans. Z, who watched the exchange, gave Trent a shrug and went back to his work.

Once all the checks were done Lexy looked at Z.

"Are you ready?"

"Let's do this."

"Khunda, open Comms to the whole ship."

"Communications open, Captain."

Lexy took a deep breath. "Ladies and gentlemen, all pre-flight checks are done and we'll be taking off shortly. Please make sure all loose items are secured before securing yourself into one of the harness chairs. We will be taking off in the next five minutes. Thank you for your cooperation. Com off."

Trent watched as Lexy, Apaleo and Z began to buckle themselves in. He followed their lead. Once Lexy's harness was secured she began typing on the console.

"Khunda, please begin take off procedures."

A deep bellowing sound came from somewhere deep in the heart of the ship. Khunda begin to mark off each of the procedures: Engines: started, Life support: functioning, artificial gravity: functioning, Life form checks in progress, twenty life forms accounted for, ground crew is cleared for take-off, flight plans have been cleared.

Z had also been typing away on the console."

"Captain," he said, "we're ready for take-off on your mark."

"Khunda, we're ready for take-off."

The ship gave a jolt and began to vibrate. The last time Trent was on the Khunda during takeoff he was knocked unconscious. The screen on the bridge showed them rising into the air and turning so that they caught a glimpse of the massive city before all they saw was deep blue space glittering with stars. The ride became smoother once they were out of the planet's atmosphere. There was a low hum from the engines that propelled them forward. It would take Khunda three hours to reach the jump port that would transport them to the Libra constellation, where the Royal children were trained to become Royal leaders.

Z stayed on the bridge to make sure there weren't any surprises on the first leg of their journey. Apaleo took Trent to the cargo bay for more training, while Lexy returned to her quarters to work on her latest book. The first hour she spent typing away, but by the second hour her hands were sore and her back was stiff. She figured the best way to work out the stiff joints was to do a short yoga practice. She stood up from the high backed armchair, pressing her palms into her lower back and arching. She reached behind the chair and grabbed a long purple mat, unrolling it on the floor.

"Khunda, can you please play some calming ocean sounds?"

The relaxing sound of waves reached her ears as she kicked off her shoes and began to ease into each pose. As it did every time she practiced, her breath slowed and deepened. She let her muscles relax. As she moved, she remembered the first time she'd ever tried yoga with the Dalai Lama. Somehow he had managed to talk her into it. She still was not quite sure how, but she was grateful. He was a very easy man to open up to even though Lexy wasn't the type to open up so easily. They had a long conversation about what she did on Earth. He seemed to be genuinely interested in her writing, but as she explained to him, it was a source of great stress because not only did she have to keep up appearances, she also had to keep up with all her work for the CTA. The rise in piracy and the rebellions that kept popping up began to make each mission more difficult.

She ended her practice as she always had, by meditating. She closed her eyes, placed her hands on her knees and focused on the simple act of inhaling and exhaling. She wasn't quite sure how much time passed, but it felt as if she was waking from a deep rest. She began to wiggle her fingers and her toes and slowly stretch out each limb. After rolling up her mat and sliding her shoes back on, she was ready to take on the Royal mission and, hopefully, there wouldn't be any unplanned situations.

Khunda

Chapter Fourteen

When Lexy returned to the bridge, Trent was sitting in her chair. He and Z were laughing. Trent stood immediately.

"You don't have to move, I can sit over here," she said, motioning to the navigation chair.

"How's the flight going?"

"So far, uneventful and boring as hell," Z replied.

"Well, we can't always run into mercenaries," Lexy said, pulling up reports on the navigation monitor.

"Really? Because we have on the last four missions."

Trent looked shocked by this.

"Wait, like space pirates?"

Z snorted. "As real as your mom's vag-"

"Z! I thought you were going to try to be less

vulgar for this one?" Lexy snapped.

"I said try. That doesn't mean I'm going to turn into a monk."

Trent chuckled.

"And you don't need to be encouraging his behavior," Lexy said, narrowing her eyes at Trent.

Khunda's voice interrupted them. "Captain, we are arriving at the first jump point."

"Trent, switch places with me."

She buckled herself into the Captain's chair and Trent followed her example in the navigator seat.

"Khunda, please send our documents to the jump station and alert the crew we are about to jump."

A green light flashed in the center of the console. Z and Lexy exchanged looks.

"Do we have to talk to these bastards every time we want to-" Lexy slapped her hand over Z's mouth as a face appeared on the screen.

"Captain Lexy Gregg's, funny seeing you here."

The screen filled with the face of Captain Marcus Zetha of the transport ship Wonder.

Lexy's face dropped and Z shoved her hand away from his mouth.

"You have got to be fucking shitting me!"

"Always a warm welcome with you, Z."

"Hello Captain Zetha. If you don't mind me asking, why are you here?"

Lexy's voice sounded forced, even to her. Zetha's eyes met hers and her heart began to thump in her ears. Even when Lexy hated him he still managed to make her flush.

"I am currently transporting a group of religious leaders that will be attending the Royal celebrations."

"Shit," Z sat back with his arms crossed.

Zetha gave Z a not so friendly stare. Lexy was at a loss for words.

"Captain Zetha, my name is Officer Trent. It's a pleasure to meet you."

Trent didn't like the way Zetha's eyes lit up.

"Well… well… this is the infamous Earthling stowaway."

Z dropped his forehead into his hand as Lexy pinched the bridge of her nose.

"That's enough chit chat for now. If you don't mind, we have important business to attend to, in case you haven't heard," Z said, slapping his hand on the console to end the communication feed.

"Z! What the hell? You just hung up on him."

"He's a douche."

"That douche could file a complaint against you."

"Ha! Let him. It's been a while since I got a complaint."

Lexy laughed. "You're an idiot."

Trent was still standing. "How does he know about me?"

Z swung his chair around to face Trent. "As for you hot shot, the unenlightened earthling, meaning you, is not allowed to talk, capish?"

Trent sat down. "Got it."

Lexy felt sorry for him. He was being reprimanded by a gray half his size for introducing himself, which would've been completely normal on Earth.

"Z, don't take your frustration out on him. Trent, a screw-up like an unenlightened stowaway is not something you can keep secret at the CTA. It's not your fault either, that's on me. Khunda, is the damn jump ready?"

"Yes, Captain, the damn jump is ready."

Silence filled the bridge, which was broken when Z and Trent could no longer hold back their laughter.

Lexy shook her head. "Remind me to adjust her learning parameters."

The ship eased toward the jump circle, bolts of lightning shot across the metal outline. Z began his usual countdown and the Khunda sped toward the center. In a blink of an eye they were shot across space to the Libra galaxy.

An hour later Lexy was hiding in her quarters, trying to hash out the final scene in her new book. She was frustrated and taking it out on her characters. She stopped typing and pushed her laptop to the side, dropping her forehead onto the cool countertop. There were times when writing was a fulfilling and creative experience, but there were also times like this when it made life more frustrating. Lexy was trying to think about how she could wrap up her story in a nice little bow when a knock at the door brought her head up with a snap.

"Come in," she eased her laptop closed.

Trent stepped into the room, hands in his pockets.

"Hey, I just thought I would stretch my legs."

"And you're legs took you here?"

"Uh- I guess so," he stuttered.

A short silence sat between them.

"So I guess I'll go." He turned to leave.

"No, come back in. I'm just in a bitchy mood."

"I wasn't going to say it to your face."

"Don't make me change my mind." She stood to stretch her back.

"How's your first space trip going?"

"Technically, this is my second one. I just wasn't conscious for the first one."

Lexy narrowed her eyes at him. "Do you want anything to drink?"

"No thanks."

She picked up her cup of tea that had grown cold

and placed it behind a sliding door next to the stove; five seconds later it was steaming.

"How's Apaleo treating you?"

"Like I'm a stupid Earthling."

Lexy laughed.

Trent was staring out the long window behind the couch at the millions of stars in the distance.

"It's beautiful, isn't it?"

"It's insane how big it is out here. Are they all inhabited?" he asked.

"No, not all of them." Lexy stood next to him taking in the view.

Trent broke the silence with a question Lexy wasn't sure how to answer.

"How does a planet become enlightened?"

Lexy sipped her tea, choosing her words carefully.

"First, they have to prove that they're not only technologically advanced, but also that they have a high value for life. Not just the main species, but all life. Then, the committee sends 'spies', I guess you could call them, to gather information and bring it back. The committee goes over all this information and based on what they discover, decides whether or not to send messengers. The process can take centuries."

Trent crossed his arms, his eyebrows pinched together. "So a committee decides the fate of an entire planet?"

Lexy looked at his face to see if it was anger she detected in his voice. "Basically, but what you have to understand is the committee isn't just anyone. It's made up of leaders chosen from every species. The committee began centuries ago because they used to let any advanced planet into enlightenment. Then wars broke out. Several planets were destroyed. So many lives were lost. So, they decided the main factor had to be a respect for life."

Trent relaxed a little bit, leaning back to sit on the side of the couch. He let out a deep sigh and met Lexy's eyes. "It's a lot to take in and it's terrifying to think about with all this out here," his hand waved at the window. "Earth could be invaded or attacked because another species doesn't like that we were created."

Lexy looked at her tea. "I know this is hard for you. I've had my entire life to get used to this. You've had barely forty-eight hours." Lexy traced the CTA logo on her cup. "I'm trying to get through this mission without any issues. The Royals, while smart and great at running planets for the greater good, are also spoiled brats who could end my career in a heartbeat. I need this mission to go well, and if you help me with that, I promise I will tell you everything I know about the universe and its history. I even have my notes from the academy," Lexy said, sticking her hand out.

"Do we have a deal?"

Trent stood, taking her hand. Neither one of them moved. Lexy's face began to burn and she could feel the heat spreading through her whole body. She let go of his hand out of fear he could feel her heartbeat. It was thumping wildly in her ears and coursing down her arms.

The silence was broken by Kaunda. "Captain, we are about to enter Alpha Libra's check points."

Lexy set her teacup on the coffee table. "I need to get back to the bridge and you need to find Apaleo. We'll be landing soon."

For Khunda to be allowed onto Alpha Libra, she had to go through two checkpoints. The first scanned her systems and assigned escort ships, much like a tugboat leading a tanker into port. The second scanned the life forms on board and collected the crew's info cards.

Once they passed the check points, Z landed the Khunda and the crew moved to the cargo bay and anxiously waited for the door to open. When Lexy stepped out of the elevator all the nervous chatter turned to hushed whispers. She stopped at the top of the stairs and looked out over her crew, reminded yet again that their careers were in her hands.

No pressure there.

She walked down the stairs and stood between Z and Apaleo, then said," Khunda, you can open the bay doors."

The sound of the seal releasing on the doors made a few of the crew members jump.

"Here we go," Lexy said under her breath.

The door met the dock and a flurry of music and cheering flooded the bay. Lexy and Z led the way, followed by Apaleo, Trent and then the rest of the crew. At the end of the dock the large crowd gathered there threw confetti and waved ribbons in the air. Standing just at the end of the dock was their contact. Lexy knew of her from history classes at the Academy. Madam Hebe was tall and elegant, with pointed ears like Ali. Her long dark hair was pulled away from her face and fashioned into braids, and her emerald eyes sparkled; lit by her smile. She was a beautiful woman with a youthful face considering she should be over seventy, at least.

Lexy reached the end of the dock and extended her hand to Madam Hebe. "Hello Madam, I am Captain Greggs of the transport ship Khunda." Lexy bowed her head. "It's a pleasure to meet you."

A wide smile spread across the Madam's face. "My dear Captain, the pleasure is all mine." She placed a finger under Lexy's chin and lifted until their eyes met, "Such a lovely face. You look so much like a sister of mine."

This made Lexy's cheeks burn.

The Madam took Lexy by the arm, directing her

up the walkway. "Captain, I have been given every assurance by your director that you will deliver our dear Edward safely to his new home."

"Yes, Madam Hebe, I take my job seriously and my job is to deliver the prince safely to his seat on Alpha Virgo."

Lexy allowed herself to be led by the Madam, who began chatting away about the history of the Royal Academy. The rest of the crowd, including her crew, followed. The path wound its way past beautiful gardens and greenhouses covered in plant life.

"When I started here as just a teacher, these green houses were in terrible shape. But, of course, I insisted as a part of their education, the young Royals should learn to maintain the grounds…"

Once they reached the top of the hill Lexy could see the stone castle where the Royal children lived and studied. Lexy had never been to Alpha Libra, but she could see why it was the perfect place for the future leaders.

"Several guard posts are set up in the woods surrounding the grounds as well as in the tallest towers in the castle," the madam explained, as Lexy took in the grounds.

The sprawling land offered a sense of freedom while the castle inspired a sense of duty. The stone castle looked just ones she had seen in pictures on Earth.

Maybe this is where they got the idea for them.

Lexy knew that beings had visited Earth since the terraforming, and many of Earth's cultures were shaped by the visitors.

The group walked through the large entry doors. Lexy took in the cavernous entryway.

"To the left is the grand ballroom where we shall have our ball tonight, and to the right is the most comprehensive library in all the known worlds, if I may say so" the madam said with a smile.

The ceiling reflected the constellations in the night sky. The columns that lined both sides of the entryway were carved with the likeness of the known ancients. Hestia, Demeter and Hera to the left, while Poseidon, Zeus and Apollo lined the right side. The madam led Lexy forward toward two staircases that arose in opposite directions. Between them was a set of doors.

"This, my dear Captain, is the common room where we shall take our meal."

The doors opened and Lexy was awestruck at the room before her. Fireplaces large enough to stand in took up the walls to her left and right. Inviting couches and high back chairs formed a semicircle around each fireplace. In front of her stood a wall lined with floor-to-ceiling windows. Between each of the windows sat a table with four chairs. The Madam walked to the center of the room and when she reached a large table laden with various foods, she turned to face the crowd.

"I welcome the crew of Khunda and hope you enjoy your stay at the academy. Please enjoy this meal and feel free to explore the grounds."

In turn, the crew of the Khunda shook hands with the madam and thanked her for the hospitality before loading their plates with food. Lexy made her plate and found a table in the corner next to a window. Z, with a large cup full of green juice, took the seat across from her.

"Holy crap Lex, did you see that spread! They really know how to roll out the red carpet."

Trent took the seat next to Z, setting down his plate of salad, veggies and a roll before pulling his chair up to the table. Z made a funny face.

"Is that what you're going to eat?"

Trent shrugged, "I wasn't sure about the choice of meat products."

Z let out a snort, "Then you don't want to ask what's in the soup."

Lexy took a sip of her tea. "After we eat I want to walk through the gardens. Anyone with me?"

"Do plants here bite?"

Z gave Trent a sideways glance. "Dude, you got issues," he said, then chugged the last of his juice before wandering off to get more.

Lexy moved her food around her plate, lost in

thought.

"Lexy?"

Trent's voice pulled her out of her reverie. "Yeah I'm fine. I was just thinking that we should have been introduced to the prince at the dock."

"That's what Apaleo said."

As if he heard his name across the room, Apaleo stood from his solitary seat and walked over to their table, taking the chair next to Lexy.

"Our schedules said that we would meet the prince before our meal," he whispered.

Lexy gave him a weak smile. "That's what we were just talking about. What do you think is going on?"

"I'm not sure, but there are rumors that this prince is a bit more unruly and independent than those that came before him."

"Lucky us," Trent said, sniffing a piece of broccoli before eating it.

Lexy's eyes grew wide as she took in Apaleo's face, "People tell you rumors?"

Stone-faced, he turned to her and said, "No. I overheard the maids talking about it during landing."

"Oh, that makes more sense." She took a bite of a pumpkin pastry.

Z sat down with two large glasses, one filled with green juice, one with red. "What did I miss?"

"Nothing, we were just wondering if we were going to meet our cargo before takeoff." Lexy said, pushing her empty plate to the middle of the table.

Z finished chugging the red juice and dropped his cup on the table. He wiped his lips with the back of his hand. "Ah, you know these Royals. He's probably off playing hide the pickle with as many people as he can find."

Lexy and Apaleo scowled at him.

"What?" Z shrugged.

The sound of someone clearing their throat came from behind him. "I assure you our prince is simply unavailable at the moment."

Realization slid across Z's face.

Lexy sat straight in her chair. "Yes Madam, I believe our pilot was-"

"I take no offense to the comment, my dear Captain; we all know how the Grays can be."

Z's jaw dropped open but he wouldn't dare comment back. The madam turned on her heel and walked a few tables away from them.

"Really?! No one could have warned me?" Z huffed.

Lexy threw a leftover piece of bread hitting Z in the forehead. "If you could control your mouth we wouldn't have to warn you."

Lexy stood, pushing her chair back. "I'm going to

walk through the gardens."

Z finished his drink and followed Lexy, while Trent stayed seated, tapping his fingers on the table.

Apaleo raised an eyebrow. "Let's go."

Trent and Apaleo followed after Z and Lexy.

They spent an hour wandering through greenhouses filled with vegetation from various planets and admiring the water fountains built at the four corners of the castle, Later, they found themselves lost in a hedge maze. Z was currently leading them, exclaiming every five minutes that he was a pilot and had an internal compass. Trent kept asking Z if they were there yet and Lexy threw small twigs at the back of Z's head. Apaleo was several feet behind the group, annoyed that he had come.

"Are we there yet?"

"Shut your mouth newbie, I know exactly where we're going."

"Yeah. But are we there yet?"

Z turned, climbed up onto the nearest planter so that he was face-to-face with Trent. "Hey, asswipe, you don't want to piss me off."

Z and Trent did a horrible job of keeping straight faces as they yelled absurdities at each other. Lexy rolled her eyes and continued walking around the corner in front of them. Before her was a small greenhouse with rose bushes growing up the sides. Lexy was in awe of the beautiful red and white blossoms covering the vines. She walked forward, eyeing the largest white flower, and upon reaching it, cupped it in her hand. She leaned forward to smell it and out of the corner of her eye, noticed movement inside the greenhouse. At that moment she heard Trent and Z walk up behind her, still arguing. With her face still close to the rose she slung her arm behind her, signaling them to be quiet. Z walked up next to her and found a small opening in the vines that he could peek through. Trent did the same. The three of them peered into the greenhouse to try and make out what the movement was.

"Oh crap," Lexy jerked her head back in realization of what she was seeing, and then clapped her hand over her mouth to stifle her laughter.

Trent pulled his head back next, eyes wide, trying to keep a straight face. After some time, Z still had his nose pressed against the glass. Lexy leaned over and slapped him on the shoulder.

"What? If you don't want people to watch, you shouldn't be doing it in a glass building."

Trent shrugged. "Do you think it's the prince?"

"Another stupid question from the newbie. If you were getting ready to be shipped off the planet wouldn't you try to get some before you left?" Z asked.

Apaleo walked up behind Lexy and, looking over her shoulder, he regained his posture and then shook his head. "That's not sanitary," he said, walking to the opening across from where they had come from.

Lexy and Trent followed, while Z pressed his nose against the glass again.

"Z! Get over here," Lexy yelled over her shoulder.

They found their way out of the maze and returned to the castle where they were each escorted to separate rooms to get ready for the ball. Lexy's room had a large four-poster bed, fireplace and balcony overlooking the lake where the Khunda was parked. When she entered the room there was a tub filled with warm water smelling like rose oil. She undressed and slipped into the tub. She had a good ten minutes of quiet before someone knocked on the door. Three ladies walked in without waiting for her to respond. The first held a tray with what looked like soaps and salts, the second girl's tray had jewelry on it, and the last girl was carrying a royal blue gown that she draped across the bed.

"Thank you," Lexy said, sinking lower into the bath.

The girls began to busy themselves with various tasks. The one with the soaps and salts knelt down next to the tub. Lexy eyed her cautiously. The girl wrapped a bar of soap in a white piece of linen and proceeded to dunk it in the water just above Lexy's knees. She instinctively grabbed the girl's wrist, startling her.

"I can clean myself, thank you."

The girl nodded, stood and began mixing the salts. "May I pour these in?"

Lexy felt bad for startling her. "Yes, that's fine,"

The girls helped Lexy get ready. They braided her hair and helped her into the gown. She didn't have time to look in the mirror before she was swept out of the room. The girls pushed her in the direction of the main staircase and left with their hands over their mouths, whispering to each other. Lexy felt awkward and out of place. Dresses were not her thing. She walked down the long hallway and took a right which led her to the top of the main staircase.

The entrance hall was full of beings, from Royals to staff members balancing trays of food and drinks for the guests. Z was standing at the top of the stairs with the two maids, an officer, Apaleo and Trent, all standing in a circle. He whistled when he noticed her.

"Damn Lexy, why don't you wear nice things like that for me?"

This made the other members of the group look at her. Her cheeks burned and she dropped her gaze to the floor. She never liked being the center of attention. When she looked back up she noticed the maids were each wearing beautiful gowns and the men were wearing formal CTA uniforms.

She joined them, smiling. "You all look very nice."

Apaleo's face said that he didn't enjoy the formal wear either. "We should go down before they think we are being unfriendly."

Lexy waited for the group to go ahead of her. She noticed Trent was doing the same.

"If you tell my aunt about this she will start buying me dresses. So, if you want to get home I suggest you keep your mouth shut."

Trent's mouth pulled in the corner. "All I was going to say is that you look nice, and ask if I could walk you down."

He stuck out his arm and Lexy wrapped her arm around his. As they walked down the stairs, Lexy focused on her steps in fear that at any moment she was going to trip and take out everyone in front of her. However, they made it to the entryway without injury. Waiters wove through the crowd with trays of a rose colored drink. A tall blue waiter held out his tray to Trent, who looked questioningly at Lexy. She explained that it was the equivalent of champagne. Trent took a glass and handed it to Lexy before taking one for himself. They were joined by Z and Apaleo. Z nudged the waiter's side.

"Don't forget the little people. We drink too."

"Z, could you try to not get drunk tonight?"

"I will have you know that we grays have a very fast metabolism and these are pansy drinks. I couldn't get drunk on these if I chugged a whole barrel."

Lexy's face twisted in disapproval.

"Oh come on. I can't be sober for this shit," he motioned to the room full of Royal socialites.

"Fine, but no double fisting," Lexy warned.

Trent snorted into his glass as Z downed the drink he was holding as if it was a shot, and then switched out the empty glass for a full one. They made their way through the crowd into the ballroom. Once inside, they spotted Madam Hebe near a raised platform in the middle of the room. When she saw them, she threw her arms open.

"Here they are! Such fine specimens," she looked Apaleo up-and-down. He tugged at the hem of his sleeves.

"Please my dears, stand here with me. Edward should be introduced any moment now," she said, placing herself next to Apaleo.

They made small talk for a few moments before a man walked onto the platform. The room fell silent.

"Ladies and gentlemen, I present the future king of the Virgo Constellation, Prince Edward of the Alpha Leo Royal bloodline."

The crowd clapped and a few of the royals in training cheered and cat-called from the back of the room. People moved out of the way as Edward entered the ballroom and walked onto the platform. From where she was standing Lexy could see he was in his early twenties, handsome, with light brown hair and piercing blue eyes. She looked around at her crew. The female members were huddled together giggling and looking Edward up and down. Lexy made a mental note to have a chat with them about not doing anything stupid. The Prince seemed to be enjoying the applause and cheers, and bowed and waved until Madam Hebe joined him on the platform.

She held her hand up, silencing the room. "My dear guests, today is a day of great mixed emotions. On one hand I am overjoyed that one of my best students has been selected to be the King of Alpha Virgo. On the other hand, our dear Edward shall be leaving us."

She placed her hand over her heart with one hand and gave Edward a small hug with the other.

"But enough gushing over this bright young man. Let me introduce to you the crew of Khunda who will be transporting our dear Edward to his destination."

She waved for the crew to join her. Z pressed his hand into Lexy's lower back forcing her to step up first. She could feel her face burning as she climbed the steps.

"I am very pleased to present Captain Lexy Greggs, her pilot Zefron of Alpha Orion, head of security Apaleo of the Aries tribe and the rest of the crew."

The whole crew stepped onto the platform. The

crowd gave them the appropriate amount of applause. Lexy was grateful that it didn't last too long. While she searched for the fastest escape route off the platform her eyes met someone familiar. Captain Marcus was leaning against the wall near the door. He smiled, his eyes locked on hers.

Oh good, someone else to avoid, she thought angrily.

Madam Hebe held up her hand once again to silence the crowd. "Please enjoy the food, the dancing and, of course, the drinks."

A rumble of laughter came from the crowd as Lexy turned to walk off the platform, but Madam Hebe took her by the arm and directed her back to face Edward.

"My dear Captain may I introduce you to Prince Edward of Alpha Leo- oops. I meant to say the future King of Alpha Virgo," the madam said.

Lexy smiled and held out her hand. Edward took it, and while keeping eye contact, he bent down and kissed it, then said, "My sweet Madam Hebe, you did not tell me our Captain was such a beauty."

Oh, he is good. Definitely have to talk to the staff before takeoff.

"Thank you," Lexy said and pulled her hand back, turned and rejoined the group.

She spent most of the evening meeting wealthy and powerful beings from all over the Royal planets. While discussing the increase in piracy in the Draco constellation, Lexy felt a light tap on her shoulder. She turned, hoping it was someone who didn't want to enslave whole planets for their own benefit. She was face-to-face with Marcus. *Damn*.

"Lexy, I've been trying to catch you alone all night."

"Funny, because I have been avoiding you all night."

She turned to walk away but noticed Edward walking toward her, eyes locked on her.

"Shit," she turned to Marcus, narrowing her eyes, "How about a dance?"

"I thought you-" he started.

Lexy grabbed him by the arm and dragged him to the dance floor. He slid his hand behind her back. The two began to dance awkwardly, both staring in opposite directions.

"Congratulations on the mission," he said, without looking at her.

"Thank you, Captain Zetha."

"My name is Marcus, Lexy. Please, use my name. You don't need to be so formal with me."

Lexy let out a snort, staring over his shoulder she watched Trent dance with a Royal student. She was wearing a blue sash that identified her as being eligible for testing.

"I see you have a new security officer." Marcus

sounded upset.

"Yep."

Silence filled the small space between them.

"So you pick up a hitchhiker and the director gives him job?"

"Christ, I knew you just wanted to rub that in my face."

Lexy tried to pull away from him, but he pulled her into him harder.

"Lexy, I'm not trying to have it out. I just think it's strange that the director gave him the job of protecting a future King, your crew, and you, and he just happened to jump aboard your ship."

Lexy could feel her face burning and this time it wasn't because people around them were staring.

"That is none of your business. I trust the director, not to mention she's my boss; I can't tell her no."

"Yes, you can-" he started.

"No, I can't." Lexy sucked in a gulp of air, letting it out slowly. "Look, I can't do anything about this so I'm trying to get through my mission. What do you care anyway? You would love to get rid of me; then you could be the best the CTA has to offer."

They had stopped dancing and were standing in the middle of the dance floor with their arms crossed.

"That's not true Lexy, and you know it." He

turned and walked out of the ballroom.

He can't walk away from me.

Lexy followed him; anger boiling up inside of her with every step. In the main entrance she searched the room. She rose up onto the balls of her feet to look over the crowd. She saw him walk into the common room. Grabbing a handful of her skirt she rushed after him. In the common room several groups were gathered around the fireplaces, most likely discussing politics. Many of the chair's occupants sat in relaxed positions, most likely discussing money. Marcus walked out one of the windows that had been opened for the ball. Lexy followed. The windows opened to a large stone patio with stairs on either side leading into the gardens. Her eyes narrowed when she found Marcus leaning on the railing in front of her.

"I knew you couldn't resist me," a devilish grin spread across his face.

She stormed up to him, rose onto her toes so that they were eye to eye. "You are such an asshole. Why are you even here?"

"I have a mission."

"I don't give a shit about your mission. You know what I think? I think you begged for a mission that would put you on the Royal tour and you know why I think you did it? I think you did it just so you could screw up my mission." She emphasized her last words with a smug nod.

"Lexy, you could not be more wrong." He leaned forward so they were almost touching, "But I'm really enjoying you being angry. It's like that time you and I were stuck on-."

Lexy dropped back on her heels to create some more space between them, "Why is it always about sex with you?"

"As I recall, you really enjoyed that part, too." He stepped forward to close the space between them, wrapping his arm around her back and pushing her into him.

"That was a mistake." Lexy began to panic, her heart was racing and she could feel her lower body warming.

He leaned closer and put his lips near her ear and whispered, "Maybe the first time, but what about every time after that?"

Lexy's eyes rolled into the back of her head. It had been a long time since someone was this close. Marcus' hand slid along her cheek and she opened her eyes to meet his. Before she knew what was happening his lips were on hers. She let out a small moan. His arms wrapped around her while his tongue searched her mouth. He always was good at this part.

WAS. He WAS always good at this part. It was everything else in the relationship he sucked at. Wake up, Lexy! Don't let him win.

Lexy leaned back, breathing heavily, her hands

pushing on his chest, "No. I'm not doing this again."

Marcus stood silently staring at her. She had pushed her way free, grabbed a handful of skirt and headed back inside. She wasn't paying attention to where she was going and walked straight into someone.

"Sorry, I-"

It was Trent who is standing just inside the window.

"Trent, I-"

Trent stood to one side giving her space to pass him.

"You were just getting some air."

Lexy looked from Trent to Marcus, knowing that he had seen what just happened. She shook her head. *I can't deal with this right now.*

"Good night, Trent," Lexy said and continued on her way.

She left the common room and climbed the stairs, grateful that the corridor was empty. Before she reached her room she heard a rustling noise to her right. She stopped and looked around to see if anyone else was in the hall. The noise was coming from a small library. The door sat slightly open, just enough space for her to slip her head in and look toward the sound. The prince was pressing a woman against the wall. Her dress pulled up to her waist; his shirt in a crumpled heap on the floor. Lexy removed her head from the doorway and rushed to her room. She quietly closed the doors and leaned against them. Her heart was beating so fast it made her dizzy. Her mind raced as she thought about everything that had transpired this evening. *Does everyone have sex on their mind?*

Chapter Fifteen

Lexy woke the next morning stiff and achy. She rolled onto her side and came face-to-face with Z.

She jumped up. "What the hell is wrong with you, Z?"

"I just wanted to see if Captain fancy pants took you to his room or if you took him to yours."

Lexy fell face first into her pillow, "I don't want to talk about this."

Z ignored her muffled response. "Shit Lexy, I thought we talked about this. You said you were over him. Actually I believe your exact words were 'what the fuck was I thinking? I am so over him. If I ever do anything that stupid again I give you permission to drop my ass in a black hole.' Or something like that." Z waved his hand through the air.

Lexy sat up. "Well, after this mission you can

drop me off in a black hole."

She got out of bed, grabbing her uniform that was draped over a chair and walked behind a curtain to change.

"Lexy, I'm serious. Do you remember what happened last time you got involved with fancy pants?"

Lexy stuck her head out from behind the curtain. "First off, we are not involved. He kissed me and that's all it was. I pushed away and came back to my room…alone."

Z propped himself on his elbow. "Explains why you seem a little bit… frustrated."

Lexy walked out from behind the curtain to throw her PJs at him. "I'm not frustrated. I'm annoyed, and Marcus-," Z raised his eyebrow at her, "I mean Captain Zetha has nothing to do with it. Guess who I saw doing the dirty in the library on my way back to my room?"

Z kicked his feet off the bed. "Colonel Mustard?"

Lexy snorted. "The Prince."

"Seriously? Well good for him." He hopped off the bed. "Got to get your rocks off when you can." Z reached for the doorknob.

"Freeze." Lexy yelled, "What did you do last night?"

"Oh, you know just kicking it with my homie's."

"Z! Please tell me it wasn't a member of our crew."

"Okay. It wasn't a member of our crew." Z

opened the door and walked into the hallway.

Lexy grabbed her jacket and followed him. "No really, Z, tell me it wasn't someone on our crew."

"Lexy I don't think I can tell you that with a straight face."

They argued their way to the common room where breakfast was being served. Lexy loaded up a plate with eggs, toast and grabbed a cup of hot tea. She looked around and found a table near an open window. Taking in the fresh air, she looked out past the patio and over the grounds, watching as a member of the guard walked into the tree line, *must be shift change.*

Someone sat in the seat across from her.

"I want to apologize," Marcus stated.

"For what?" She knew several reasons he should be apologizing. "For cheating on me? For lying to me? Or for kissing me last night when you know I hate you?"

"All of it. I was stupid and I-," He reached for her hand, but she slid it into her lap, "I know now that I screwed up the best thing that has ever happened to me. I know that we were only together for a few months but in that time I-"

"I don't want to hear about it. I've moved on." Lexy shoved a fork full of eggs into her mouth and returned to staring at the tree line.

Z sat down next to Marcus. "That seat is taken, asswipe."

Marcus looked like he was going to respond when Trent walked up to him. "That's my seat."

Z winked at Marcus. "Told ya."

Trent slid his plate onto the table as Marcus stood. They looked at each other for a moment. Marcus put his hand on Trent's shoulder. "Good to see you again." He smiled and walked away.

"Cocky shithead, isn't he? I bet he has a few unsavory stops planned for his cargo," Z went on, unaware Lexy wasn't listening, "I heard his cargo brought their wives and their girlfriends. Talk about friction-"

Lexy cleared her throat, "I have to check some things before takeoff."

She stood to leave and Trent stood with her. "I'll come with you."

Lexy nodded.

They left Z, his mouth hanging open, at the table.

Trent and Lexy walked silently along the path leading to the docks. Lexy was trying to focus on the mission, but Marcus' face kept gliding into her mind. Finally her frustration boiled over.

"He has the audacity to kiss me last night and try to apologize for everything at breakfast. While we are on a Royal mission. He has to be trying to get into my head. That's it; he just wants to screw me up so he can get his third star before me. Z is right; he is a shit head."

Trent stopped walking.

"Sorry. I just hate that I let him get into my head like that," she said.

"So, you and he…" Trent trailed off.

Lexy nodded, "We dated for a few months and then I found him with someone else…well, two someone else's."

Trent scratched his neck. "Do you want me to kick his ass or something?"

"No," Lexy laughed, "I should have known better. He has helped us out of some tight spots, but he can be a playboy."

They started walking again. "It's not your fault," Trent said. "He was the one that chose to cheat."

"I know. I just can't believe I was that stupid."

They walked in silence the rest of the way. Lexy felt better. *I can't let Marcus get into my head. Ameran chose us for this mission and I am not going to let anyone screw this up.*

On the Khunda they began preparations for take-off. Lexy was hiding on the bridge as all of the crew members began to arrive. Luckily everyone was preoccupied, preparing for Edward to board. Several of Edward's trunks were brought aboard. Some were taken to his room while others were loaded into the storage room behind the jump ship. It was still early and most of the crowd gathering at the end of the dock were dragging their feet and blocking the light from their eyes. Z joined Lexy on the bridge, placing a wadded up cloth napkin on the console next to her. She looked from the napkin to Z and cautiously peeled back the layers. Wrapped inside was a small scone, Lexy's favorite.

"I assumed you didn't get one, so I snagged one for ya."

Lexy smiled at him and broke the scone in half. "Thank you." She handed one half to Z and then said, "Let's go welcome the prince aboard."

They left the bridge, each eating their half of the scone.

"Just think Lexy, twenty-four hours from now this horn dog Prince will be on his planet and out of our hair. And we'll be the rock stars of the CTA."

The elevator doors opened to the cargo bay, "I don't want to be rock stars. I just don't want to get fired."

"The director would never fire us she loves us."

"Really? We just had to get a new jump ship because you pissed off of a mercenary and he shot a hole through it. Do you really think she wouldn't fire us?"

"That wasn't my fault."

Lexy stopped at the top of the stairs, staring at Z.

"Okay, it was a little bit my fault, but you helped." Z shook his head. "Insulting his mother. Whoever thought that was a good idea?"

Most of the guests from the ball had come out to say goodbye to the prince. Lexy had to give him credit; he graciously shook every hand and kissed every lady on the cheek. Once the fanfare was over he walked into the cargo bay and began introducing himself to the crew. Lexy shook Madam Hebe's hand.

She said, "You get him to his coronation on time, my dear, and you will always be welcome here at the academy."

Lexy smiled, "He will be there."

She walked back into the cargo bay as the large door closed behind her. "Hermes, would you be so kind as to show the prince his quarters during takeoff."

"My dear captain, I figured I would be taking my place on the bridge with you."

Lexy kept a smile on her face. "Sorry, your highness, but there is no room on the bridge."

He shrugged and turned to face Hermes. "This is a smaller vessel than I am used to. My father's fleet never had such a quaint ship. I guess we must listen to our captain; show me the way young man."

Lexy pretended not to hear him, waiting until they were in the elevator before addressing the rest of the crew. "Everyone, we are now on the clock. I expect your best, and in return, I will get you to our destination safely.

So, let's get ready for takeoff."

The crew headed to the elevators in silence.

They must be nervous too.

Once they were out of the planet's orbit, Lexy and Z went to the common room for lunch. After getting their food they sat down in their usual spot in the corner. Trent walked in shortly after, got his tray and sat in the chair Lexy pushed out next to her. Trent winked at her, making her cheeks burn. She smiled, forcing herself to focus on her food. Z noticed the exchange but knew better than to comment. Apaleo took the seat across from Trent. Every table was chattering away, while theirs was silent.

Lexy was about to excuse herself when Anuke, one of the stewards, rushed off the elevator, short of breath. Lexy looked at him questioningly. He gave a small wave for her to follow him. He stepped back onto the elevator, followed by Lexy, Z, Apaleo and Trent.

"What's wrong, Anuke?" Lexy looked at him, worried.

Anuke stuttered as if he was searching for the right words. "W-well, captain…I was g-going to see if the prince wanted anything t-to eat when…um…"

The doors opened and Lexy stepped out first. Her hands balled just in case. Standing in the guest common room she heard what was causing Anuke to hesitate. Muffled moans came coming from the prince's quarters. It sounded like bad porn.

"Get it girl." Z pushed past Lexy and walked up to the door.

"Z! Get your ass back here. Anuke, who is in there with him?"

Anuke shrugged.

"Thank you for letting me know. Don't tell anyone else. Ok?"

He nodded and returned to the elevator.

"Apaleo, any guesses as to who that is?"

"A sand shark being gutted?" Apaleo crossed his arms, his face skewed in disgust.

"You're no help."

Trent was standing next to Lexy. "Alice," he said.

Lexy looked at Trent, "How do you-"

"She was the only female unaccounted for at breakfast."

Apaleo looked impressed.

Z 's ear was pressed against the door. "Oh yeah, that's Alice. She is a bit of a drama queen in the sac."

Lexy pinched the bridge of her nose. She couldn't believe what she was hearing. "What- How- You know what? I don't want to know. The question is, what do we do about it?"

Trent crossed his arms. "Honestly, she wouldn't be the only person that has done it on this mission."

She faced him, "What's that supposed to mean?"

"Uh- some of the crew have been..."

"Don't tell me," Lexy raised her hand. "In this case, ignorance is bliss."

Z raised his hand. "Uh, guys."

Apaleo shifted his weight. "Maybe you should knock."

Lexy was about to respond when Z jogged back to her side. "No need, they're done."

They hadn't noticed the moaning stopped. The elevator door opened as Alice and Edward emerged from his quarters.

There was a silence before a red streak flew past Lexy and tackled Alice.

What the hell was that?

Leda, one of the maids, was currently pulling out a chunk of Alice's hair. Realization hit Lexy, *Oh, Leda was the girl in the library.*

Edward managed to side-step the action. Trent and Lexy rushed forward to pull Leda off Alice. The two were clawing at each other's faces and pulling hair. Lexy reached Leda first and tried to grab her wrist when she drew it back. Trent grabbed Alice around the waist, trying to drag her in the other direction. While Apaleo stood in front of Edward, shielding him in case anyone caught on that he was the cause of this. Lexy was having no luck trying to get a grip on Leda.

Stepping back she yelled, "As your Captain I demand you stop!"

At that moment Leda landed a right hook to Trent's face.

Trent fell back, still holding onto Alice. Lexy didn't take this well and grabbed Leda's arm, flipped her hand behind her back and bent her wrist in an unnatural way. Leda screamed in pain as Lexy used this new leverage to slam her face first onto the floor.

"Trent, you ok?"

Profanity ensued from his direction.

Lexy looked around the room to find that half of the crew was craning to get a better look.

"Don't you all have jobs to do?"

They collectively jumped and scattered.

Lexy realized that Z had pulled up a chair and was watching just a few feet away.

Lexy flicked him off with her free hand.

"What? I'm the pilot. If I get hurt who is going to fly this thing?"

"Then go fly this thing," Lexy snapped back. Z huffed and headed to the elevator with the others.

Apaleo was escorting a smug looking Edward back into his quarters.

Dick.

Trent had Alice in a hold that looked military. "Ok, are you two done? Or am I going to have to drop you off at the next jump station?"

Leda relaxed under Lexy's grip, "No, Captain."

"Alice, how about you?"

"No, Captain."

"Good. We are going to let you two up now. If either of you so much as blink in the other's direction, I will have you immediately terminated and drop your asses so fast you won't know what world you are on. Enlightened or un-enlightened. Got it?"

"Yes, Captain," they said in unison.

Trent and Lexy let go of their holds slowly, not trusting they wouldn't go right back to it.

Lexy got up and brushed off her uniform.

"Now both of you, go to your quarters and clean up. You still have jobs to do."

The girls walked silently to the elevator, rubbing their wounds.

Lexy and Trent were alone. Lexy looked at him, noticing his cheek was already turning red where he had been hit.

"Let me see that," She walked over to him, putting her hand on his uninjured cheek and turning his head so she could see better.

"I'm fine," he said. "I just need to put some ice on

it."

"Trent, don't be a baby. Let me take a look."

Their eyes met. Lexy's body began to warm as her heart began racing. He placed his hand on hers, sliding it off of his face. "I should go get some ice."

He smiled and walked back to the elevator. Lexy let out an audible sigh. *What the hell is wrong with me?*

Khunda

Chapter Sixteen

Lexy entered the bridge and Z said, "Lexy, you can't tell me that wasn't awesome."

"We're less than an hour into our mission and we've had a cat fight onboard. Between two of the crew members, no less," she responded.

Z threw his legs onto the console, leaning back in his chair. "My god, that Alice can scream. Makes a man feel good you know-"

"Z, not now… what the hell was the prince thinking? And how the hell did he get Alice to sleep with him that fast? Does she have no self-respect?"

"I know. I have to ask him how he did it."

"No you won't ask him," Lexy slapped his feet off the desk.

She was facing the window with her back to the

door and didn't notice Apaleo had walked in with Edward. "I get that this Prince-Whore is your new idol, but if I may remind you, we are not only being watched by the director, but also by the rest of the enlightened planets. If we screw up, the director will have no choice but the fire us."

Apaleo cleared his throat behind her. "Captain, the prince would like to speak to you."

Lexy closed her eyes, turning slowly. *Please don't be there. Please don't be there. Please don't be there.*

When Lexy opened her eyes Edward was standing just inside the doorway with an amused smile on his face. "Prince-whore? I don't believe I've heard that one."

"Your highness, I-"

"Don't apologize, Captain," he walked up to Lexy and took her hand. "It is I who should apologize. This is your ship and I should've respected it."

Lexy was at a loss for words. She stood there with her mouth hanging open in shock.

"If I may, I wish to make it up to you. How about I join you for dinner in your quarters and you can tell me all about how you became the first Earthling to pass the Captains ranks at the Intergalactic Flight Academy with a perfect score. I am very interested to find out how you juggle your career on Earth with your career out here."

"Um-," Lexy didn't know what to say. *How does he know so much about me?*

"I will take that as a yes. Now if you'll excuse me, I have to find the ingredients for my famous Cucurbita soup."

Edward kissed Lexy's hand and left the bridge. They were all silently confused.

It was a few moments before Lexy regained her voice. "What the hell-"

The doors reopened and Trent entered holding an ice pack to his face. "What was the prince doing on the bridge?"

Z began to laugh hysterically, doubling over in his chair. "Lexy has a date with the prince," he spit out between breaths.

Trent threw up his hands. "Damn, he's good," he said, and left the bridge.

Apaleo followed. Still looking confused, he mumbled, "Someone should get some work done. I guess it will be me."

Lexy turned and narrowed her eyes at Z. "You're an ass," she said and headed towards the door.

"Hey, I was just joking. Where are you going?"

"I have to go clean."

Lexy spent the next hour and a half scrubbing every inch of her living room. When she finished, she still didn't feel like talking to anyone so she flipped open her laptop and began typing. An hour later, someone knocked at her door.

"Who is it?"

"Z is at your door," the Khunda answered.

"Come in."

Z peeked through the doorway. "Can I come in?"

"I wouldn't have said 'come in' if I didn't want you here."

"Yeah, but I know how you can get. You'll say come in but then just as I step in the door you'll throw something at me."

"That was one time, and you deserved it."

Z thought for a moment, "Okay, that one I'll give you."

"Why are you not arguing with me?"

Z climbed up onto the stool next to her. "I came to apologize."

Lexy stared at him in disbelief. "No really, why are you here."

"Lexy, I know you're stressed out about this mission and believe it or not I am too. I just show it in a different way. You know that I've never acted seriously."

Lexy scoffed.

"After the last few missions I can see why you would be concerned with the security of our jobs-"

Lexy threw her hand up to stop him. "Did you rehearse this?"

"Hey, it's not every day you get an apology out of me. Do you want it or not?"

Lexy nodded. "Of course, please continue."

She crossed her arms and sat back in her chair, *this oughta be good*.

"Thank you." Z cleared his throat. "I'm sorry for not backing you up at the CTA in front of the director. I'm sorry I harassed you about the captain fancy pants situation. I'm sorry I didn't help stop the fight this morning, and-" his lips pinched in an effort to keep a straight face," I'm sorry I laughed about you having a date with Prince Edward."

Lexy couldn't help but laugh. "It's not a date you idiot. I guess this is how he tries to make up for the stupid shit he does. If this makes him happy and can possibly make this mission go little bit easier I am perfectly fine with eating a meal with that jerk."

Z let his legs swing. "So Trent seems like a good guy."

Lexy shrugged. "I guess, why?"

"Seeing as he may be your only friend on Earth-"

"He's not my only friend."

"Really? Name the other ones."

Lexy thought for a second, *this may be harder than it seemed*.

Z crossed his arms, leaned back in his chair and said, "And family members don't count."

"Well there's Lizzy and Carol-"

"You can't count your agent and your publisher. In fact, let's not count anyone who makes money off your books."

Lexy thought hard about this one. "Bones…"

Z dropped his head into his hands. "This is what I'm talking about Lex. I know you and I have been best friends since birth, but we are only around each other out here. You need someone who will make sure you don't work yourself to death on Earth."

"I don't work all the time."

"Really? Are you going to sit there and lie to me?"

Z reached over and tapped her laptop. "Let me guess you're almost done drafting your next book."

Lexy shut the laptop, almost catching Z's finger. "I had a lot of time on my hands. How about we talk about something else."

"Whatever."

Someone knocked on her door. "Captain, Prince Edward is here to see you."

Z slid off the stool. "I'm not sticking around to watch this."

He walked out the door waving to Edward as he passed.

Edward walked in carrying a large pot. "Where

would you like me to set this?"

Lexy directed him to the stove in the kitchen. She got two bowls and spoons out and set them on me counter top as Edward stirred the soup with a ladle. He insisted on serving her so she took a seat.

"I wanted to apologize as well for-"

"Really Captain, no apology needed. I can see how my actions have made your job more difficult. And with the kind of stress I presume you are under for this mission I can see how I seem like a spoiled… what did you call me, Prince-whore?"

Lexy blushed. "I'm really sorry about that I didn't mean it."

"You meant it. Now, can we move on to another topic? Like, I heard this ship is yours, not the agency's. How did you end up with a ship of your own? That normally takes a Captain decades to achieve."

"Both of my parents worked for the CTA and when they died protecting their cargo the agency, or the Director to be more specific, had the Khunda commissioned for me. The director was friends with my mother and apparently my mother told her I planned to become a Captain like my father."

The prince was slurping his soup, thinking this over. "That is one hell of a gift, especially to an Earthling."

Lexy let her spoon drop into her bowl. "What's

that supposed to mean?"

Edward raised his hands in surrender "I don't mean anything by it. I personally believe that Earthlings are just as capable as any enlightened species. I just know I am one of a few that believes this."

"Ameran is different. I guess that she and my mother were really good friends. She's proven herself to me by hiring several species. She shows no bias."

"Some hide behind their good deeds." Edward stood to refill his bowl.

"From what I gather, you don't have that problem." Lexy smiled to herself.

He looked at her in shock. "Was that a joke from our dear Captain?"

"I've been known to do that from time to time. Do me a favor, though, and don't tell the crew."

"I promise."

They spent the next hour talking about their childhood and studies. Lexy was beginning to understand that while reckless and with no real respect for authority, Edward took his duties and responsibility to his new planet seriously.

"My father is a great king on Alpha Leo, and when I was sent off to the Academy I swore that I would make him proud. I had been studying for the exams since I arrived. So when it was finally my time to test I felt ready. I took the test and came out with top marks. The day they told me I was going to be the new king of Alpha Virgo I couldn't wait to tell my father. I was in the hologram room waiting for the connection. I remember my palms were sweating and I felt like my chest was going to burst from the excitement. When I told him he simply shook his head and said, 'You're going to be a great king of a constellation full of gypsies and soothsayers. I wish you the best.' And then he ended the connection and I haven't heard from him since."

Lexy didn't know what to say. She looked into her soup, stirring it in slow circles. After a few moments she looked up at Edward and said, "He's an ass."

Edward choked on a spoonful of soup and his face brightened as he smiled. "Yes, he is."

Lexy reached across the space between them and squeezed his hand. "What he says no longer matters. You may be a whore, but you have the potential to be a great king to worlds that may not be the most productive when it comes to technology or politics, but these are the people that every species turns to when they need guidance, enlighten-ment or even just someone to listen to. As far as I'm con-cerned, that is more important than anything your father has done."

Edward stared at her hand on his and gave her fingers a squeeze.

"You know it's nice to talk to someone that listens. Most of the other Royals want to talk about themselves or about what they will do when they rule or listen to someone else talk about them."

He looked into her eyes. Lexy knew that look. *Oh crap.*

Edward began to lean in still holding her hand and before she knew what she was doing her free hand swung up and pressed against his forehead.

"You don't want to do that."

Edward let go of her hand, sitting back. His mouth hung open while his eyes darted back and forth. "But I thought-"

Lexy looked at the floor. "Are you playing me? Did you have this planned the whole time?"

"Not planned..."

Lexy stood, throwing her hands in the air.

Could this day get any worse?

She started pacing in front of her couch. "Here I am thinking that I misjudged you, but all you wanted to do was try to get another notch in your belt? You've got to be kidding me. First off, I am the captain of the ship that is transporting you. Secondly, I am much older than you. Then let's add in the fact that *this* is never going to happen." Lexy stopped pacing and pointed to the door. "Get out."

Edward stood and took a step toward her. "Lexy, wait. We can talk about this-"

"It's Captain Greggs, and I said get out."

Edward left the room, running his hands through his hair. Steaming, Lexy threw the bowls in the sink; she wasn't going to deal with the cleanup. *This is ridiculous. Are men incapable of keeping it in their pants?*

Khunda

Chapter Seventeen

Lexy's heart was pounding and her mind was spinning. She needed a way to release some stress and writing wasn't going to cut it. She changed into her gym clothes and snuck downstairs. Luckily, no one else was in the mood to work out so she had the whole gym to herself. Lexy walked to the far end of the gym where the punching bag sat. She wrapped her hands and began to hit the bags as hard as she could. Bruises began to form on her knuckles, but she wasn't in the mood to care. When her hands became numb, she began to kick. With each strike she felt her anger diminish. Left leg Edward, right leg Marcus, left leg Edward.

Men are stupid. Maybe I should just adopt Z's mentality and just use them for release. Maybe I don't need a man anyway. All they ever do is fuck up my life.

Over the sound of her legs hitting the bag she heard raised voices coming from the common room. Lexy tried to ignore them, but the voices grew louder. She slumped over, hugging the bag for support, her chest rising and falling from the effort. *What now?*

Leaving the gym, she saw Edward standing across from Leda and Eris, one of the security officers. Leda seemed to be upset about something, while Edward was leaning on the counter smiling about the irritation he was causing. Lexy had enough of this. Her eyes narrowed as she stormed toward them.

"What is going on?"

Leda dropped her eyes to the floor while Edward smirked and winked at Lexy.

"No one's going to answer me?" She said, hands coming to rest on her hips.

Edward crossed his arms. "This officer seems to feel it is a place to tell me who I can and cannot talk to."

Lexy pinched the bridge of her nose, squeezing her eyes shut.

"Your highness, in the amount of time I've known you I can honestly say I do not trust your intentions with my staff. If you don't mind going back to your room until dinner….." Lexy tried to keep her tone calm.

Edward stood bolt upright. "You can't ground me."

"This is my ship. Yes I can," she snapped. *So much for calm.*

"I am a royal and soon to be king. You have no authority over me."

Edward reminded Lexy of a child that had gone too long without a nap.

"Keywords in your statement are 'soon to be', as in not yet, and as you are on my ship, my authority rules. Go to your quarters!"

Edward's eyes shot open. "The director will hear about this."

Lexy threw her hands in the air. "At this point, so be it."

Edward headed for the elevator and Lexy turned her attention to her crew members. "Spread the word that the next person that allows the prince to charm them will be dropped off at the next jump station."

Leda and Eris stared at Lexy, frozen.

"Go!"

They ran to the elevator and disappeared.

Lexy stood alone in the common room. She pressed the heels of her hands into her eyes until stars flooded her vision. Her stomach began to twist as she walked onto the observation deck.

"Khunda, open the observation deck window, please?"

The room grew dark as the far wall opened, exposing the space outside. Lexy walked to the guardrail and, sitting down, she rested her chin on the bottom rail and stared out into space. Thoughts were bouncing around her mind. It was hard to believe a couple of days ago she was optimistic about this assignment, thinking this was the turning point in her career and maybe now she would be taken seriously as a Captain. Tears burned her eyes before starting a slow stream down her face. Ever since she got her Captain's Star she'd been treated as if she hadn't earned her place among the enlightened. Even when she was awarded her second star in the Guard, she was overlooked for several promotions because of her species' status. She still felt guilty that Z had been blacklisted by other Captains because he was her pilot and best friend.

The doors opened behind her. "Capt-," Trent started.

He walked in as Lexy was wiping her eyes with her sleeve. "Yes, Trent?"

"You ok?" He stood next to her.

"I'm fine. Do you need me?" she asked.

Trent crouched next to her, placing his hand on her shoulder. She shrugged it off.

Ignoring her coldness, he sat down next to her and looked out the window. "I thought about it and I hate the prince."

Lexy looked at him. She examined his face, he hadn't shaved and his cheeks were dark with a five o'clock shadow. The left side of his face was now a deep blue and purple. She nodded. "I agree," she said, turning to look out at the window again. They sat in silence and somehow it was comforting.

Lexy sighed. "I grounded the prince."

Trent burst out laughing. "You did what?"

"He apparently was trying to 'patch' things up with Leda and Eris stepped in. They had words and..." She let out a sigh, "I grounded the prince." She pressed her forehead onto the cold metal of the railing, her eyes downcast. "My career is dead."

"No, it's not. The director will understand. Z said you're like a daughter to her."

Lexy picked at her cuticles. "The prince is above the director. The council will have me banished to Earth and I will be stripped of my Stars." Fresh tears fell into her lap.

Trent shifted, looking at her. "That won't happen. Z and I won't let it. That guy is an ass and has been nothing but trouble since we met him." He put his hands on either side of her face forcing her to look him into his eyes. "Do you want me to kick his ass?"

A giggle escaped her lips. "That would be great, but I don't want you to get into trouble too."

"Whatever you want, I'm here for you, Captain."

Lexy smiled. Without thinking, she slid her arms around his neck. Trent wrapped his arms around her back. They held onto each other for a moment. Lexy pulled back, keeping her face close to his. His fingers were tracing her cheek. Her mind went blank; his breath was warm on her skin. Lexy closed her eyes, closing the space between them when a voice made her jump.

"This explains a lot," Edward said.

Fuming, Lexy jumped to her feet and stood in front of Trent whose hands were balling into fists.

"I thought I sent you to your room." Lexy crossed her arms, looking at Edward.

"You did, but-" Edward took a step toward Lexy, but then froze when Trent stepped forward. He was so close to Lexy's back she could feel his heat.

"I have a proposition," Edward said, taking a step back with his hands up.

"I am not giving you permission to sleep with anyone," she snapped.

"No, I don't want that any more. Too easy," he winked at Lexy.

Trent popped his knuckles.

"I was going through some star charts and I noticed we are close to Zuben Mu-"

"No."

"Captain, hear me out-"

"No, I am not putting my crew in a questionable situation by going to a gambeling planet planet."

"You would really watch your career disappear for let's say... a three hour stop?"

"Are you blackmailing us?" Trent sounded as if every bit of his effort was going into not punching him.

Edward grinned. "Not you. Her." He pointed at Lexy. "It's her career, her ship, her friends and her father's dream."

Lexy took a step toward him; Trent grabbed her arm.

"Look, I am just trying to help you out of a bad situation. You insulted and then confined a future King. Either I can tell the council of my harsh treatment aboard your ship, or I can get three hours of freedom and then be asleep the rest of the trip. It's up to you."

Lexy relaxed, letting his offer sink in. Trent looked from Lexy to Edward.

"You can't seriously be thinking about this?"

Trent put his hand on her shoulder, turning her to face him.

"Lexy you can't let him win. Who's to say he won't tell the council even if you do let him go to this planet?"

Lexy raised an eyebrow and turned to face Edward.

"Would you be willing to make that promise under a scan?"

"Why? Do you think I'm lying?" Edward shrugged. "Fine, but that means I can do what I want on the planet, with whom I want; no questions asked."

Lexy stuck out her hand. "I don't leave your side and it's a deal."

The prince seemed to think this over. "We have a deal, Captain." He took Lexy's hand, lingering just a little too long.

Lexy snatched back her hand in disgust.

"I'm going now to pick out a clean shirt."

He left with a wide smile on his face. Trent looked at Lexy questioningly. "Are you seriously going to give him three hours to do who knows what?"

"It was either that or let him ruin all our careers."

Lexy left the observation deck and headed back towards bridge with Trent at her heels. "Lexy, will you talk to me? Or at least Z? I don't think this is a good idea."

Lexy stopped in front of the bridge doors. "I don't think this is a great idea either, but I really didn't have a choice. You don't understand that he wouldn't just ruin my career, he'd ruin the careers of everyone on the ship. I can't be responsible for that. If there's a way out I'm going to take it. It's only a three hour stop."

Lexy and Trent entered the bridge. Z had his legs

propped up on the console, bobbing his head to music from his planet.

Lexy slapped his feet off the desk. "Music off."

The room fell silent. "We have a problem, Z."

He looked at Lexy, then Trent. "Well … is someone going to tell me what the problem is?"

Lexy paced, and then said, "I agreed to let Edward have three hours of freedom on Zuben Mu."

Z burst out laughing. "That's funny. For a second I thought I heard you say you agreed to make a three-hour stop on a gambling planet."

Trent sat down in the navigation chair. "You heard her correctly."

"Holy shit, Lexy. Why the fuck did you go and do that?"

"I had to."

"No you didn't."

"Yes. I. Did. Z, he was going to go to the Council. We would have lost our enlightened status."

Z stared at Trent, searching for some sign that this was a joke "Is this because of the chick fight? Because I thought you two we're having dinner to work that out?"

Lexy dropped into her chair. "Yeah, well that was going fine until he tried to kiss me. Then I kicked him out so he decided to hit on someone else, which one of the guys didn't like. They got into an argument and I grounded the prince."

Z's eyes flew open and he launched into a fit of uncontrollable laughter, just managing to get out, "You grounded a member of the royals?"

"That's not really helping right now." Trent said, rubbing his temples.

"No-really-what happened?" Z snorted between fits of laughter.

Z looked into Lexy's eyes and realized she was telling the truth.

"Fuck."

All three of them sat silent, allowing this to sink in.

Z was the first to break the silence. "But how do we know he won't go back on his end of the bargain?"

"He agreed to make the promise under scan."

Z thought about this for a minute. "Okay, I'm in."

Trent stood up. "Z, you can't really be okay with this."

"Look, if Lexy thinks this is …uh …the only idea, then I'm on her side. He makes the promise under scan and he can't go back on it."

Lexy walked up to Trent, placing her hand on his crossed arms. "I know you don't understand what this means, but I have to protect my crew and this is the only way. If you're not comfortable with it you can stay here with the crew and you guys can wait until we're-"

"No, I'm not waiting for you to show back up again. If you're going, I'm going."

"Ah, that's so sweet. Now can we get the scan done so we can get this shit over with?"

"Yes" Lexy returned to her seat. "Khunda, please find Apaleo and tell him he is needed on the bridge. Also, prep the scanner for a full body, all functions scan. And can you send me the possible routes for Zuben Mu?"

They finished preparations for their new course and filled in Apaleo, who didn't seem quite as upset as they expected him to be.

The entire crew was called to the common room where Lexy made the announcement that there would be a brief layover orbiting a nearby planet. Questions and concerns were silenced by explaining that it was for their safety and there was no need to worry. Then Lexy, Trent and Edward met on the observation deck to proceed with the scan.

"You know how this works. You simply state you were never mistreated or harmed on our ship by any of the crew members. That in no way are any of us to be punished for any form of negative treatment during this transport and that we all acted under your orders as future King."

"Would you like to write a script for me, Captain?"

Lexy jumped forward and was in the prince's face before anyone had time to react.

"This scan will be done to my satisfaction, or no deal."

A cocky smile spread across his face. "Let's face it, you like being this close to me."

Lexy rolled her eyes and stepped back to stand next to Trent.

"Khunda, begin scan and recording."

The room went dark and a green laser grid scanned over the prince. He did as he was told, releasing them from any claim or legal action. Once Lexy was satisfied with the results she asked Trent to walk Edward back to his quarters while she went back to the bridge.

She sat in her chair, running the plan over and over in her head. "Z, do you think this will work?"

Z turned in his chair to face her. "We already have the scan, which states that we were acting under his orders, so if anything happens, it's on him as a royal."

Lexy let out a sigh. "Yeah, but I'm worried about what will happen on the planet."

"I've been there a million times. I've never had any problems…. Well, there was that one time-"

Trent walked onto the bridge followed by Apaleo.

"The prince is in his quarters getting ready" Apaleo said, standing just inside the doorway with his arms crossed. "Are you sure about this, Captain?

"This is the only way." But she wasn't feeling so sure anymore.

Apaleo gave a nod. Lexy looked at Trent who shrugged.

"It's whatever you think; I'll be right behind you."

Lexy then turned to Z. "You know me Lex, I'm always up for a crazy idea."

Lexy gave a small smile and turned back to the console. "Alright, let's do this."

They managed to convince the guard station orbiting Zuben Eta that a small but crucial part of their ship had broken and they simply needed to orbit while members of the crew went to retrieve a new piece. Apaleo selected an officer to be in charge while they were gone. Then

Lexy, Trent, Z and Apaleo locked up the bridge and headed to the jump ship.

Z checked the jump ship's functions and set a course for Zuben Mu. Apaleo and Trent we're scanning and checking every inch of the ship to make sure it was secure. Lexy, hesitantly, sent a message to Ameran, explaining their small orbiting layover was due to a short repair that needed to be done. She knew the director would see through her lie, but Lexy was sure she wouldn't risk the mission.

Once the message was sent, Lexy began to double check the weapons supplies on the jump ship. She knew that on gambling planets, weapons were checked at the docks, but Z told her the rules weren't always followed.

Z was looking her up and down, "I think we're going to draw attention with our uniforms."

"What are you thinking?"

"I've got an idea." Z ran down the ramp and disappeared around the corner just as Edward made his way up the ramp.

"Captain," he gave a small bow.

Lexy pointed to a chair. "Sit there and don't say a word."

Trent and Apaleo walked up the ramp.

"Jump ship has been scanned and is clear, Captain," Apaleo said, his face pinching around his brow.

Lexy was about to ask him if everything was okay when Trent interrupted.

"Where did Z go?" he asked, looking around.

"I think he went to get us different clothes to wear."

Apaleo raised an eyebrow, "That's a good idea."

"Yeah, every once in a while he has one," Lexy replied, smiling.

Z returned; his arms full of clothes. "I'll drop these in room one."

Z dropped the clothes on the bed in the small room to the left in the jump ship and returned to the group.

"Alright let's get this show on the road."

Z and Lexy returned to the steering console, while Trent and Apaleo sat on either side of Edward. The ship's door closed and the Khunda's cargo doors opened to blackness spotted with distant stars. They hovered off the ground and then Z maneuvered them into space and took them to Zuben Mu, thirty minutes away. They took turns changing into the clothes Z had brought for them. Lexy was last to change, and when she emerged from the room she threw her arms up in exasperation.

"Really Z?!? This is what you picked for me?"

Lexy was wearing a tight black dress so short it barely covered her ass. Z broke out in hysterical laughter while Trent and Edward simply stared. Apaleo even found some humor in Lexy's new look.

"You look like a woman on-call," he commented through tight lips.

"Lex, that's how women dress there," Z said, wiping away a tear. "You want to fit in, don't you?"

"Yeah Captain, this is a good look for you," Edward said making a move to stand, but Trent grabbed him by the arm and forced him back into the chair.

"If any of you tell anyone about this I will kill you, not in a metaphorical way, in the I will have to find a place to hide the body kind of way."

Lexy stormed to her chair, trying to find a lady-like way to sit in her new outfit.

Once they landed on Zuben Mu, Lexy was able to strap a weapon to her inner thigh and slide a small knife on either side of her breasts. It wasn't comfortable, but it was the only option.

"Don't they have scanners that will make it impossible to sneak weapons in? Let alone use them?" Trent asked, remembering his time at the CTA.

Lexy handed him a small weapon. "Planets like these don't have scanners. They say it's because they don't have the money for them, but in reality it's bad for business."

Z was checking the power supply on his weapon. "These guys have their own set of rules anyway, so don't show any of your weapons unless you are being shot at."

Trent stared at Z across the table, not quite sure if he was joking.

Edward reached for a gun, but Lexy's hand got there first

"You don't get a weapon."

He was taken aback. "What happens if I need to protect myself?"

Lexy slipped the pistol toward Apaleo. "We are your protection."

"Well," he took in the four beings across from him, "I'm screwed."

Apaleo took the gun and holstered it under his belt. "That's the whole point, isn't it?"

Z looked at Apaleo. "Look at you learning how to be a real boy. I'm impressed."

Apaleo rolled his eyes and lead the way off the ship.

As they walked up the docks, Z pushed his way to the front of the group. "Let me do the talking. They know me here."

Lexy made a face at him. "Hey, what happens on Zuben Mu, stays on Zuben Mu."

Z walked ahead to the checkpoint at the end of the docks and began to have a lively conversation with one of the bouncers. After a bit, Z waved them over. "These three," Z waved at the men with Lexy, "Are the shipmates I was telling you about. And this beautiful young lady is mine for the week." Z winked at Lexy who replied by sliding her foot onto his toe and stepping down as she smiled.

"Any friend of Z's is a friend of mine. And as for you sexy," the bouncer took Lexy's hand in his, "when you're done with little man here, come find me. I'll show you how it's really done."

Lexy tried to keep her smile in place but she knew she wasn't doing a good job. Z wrapped his hand around her hips, pushing her towards the walkway leading to the casino

"Talk to you later guys." Z called over his shoulder.

Lexy could hear Edward snickering behind her.

"I'm setting my band, your three hours begins now." Lexy told Edward as he caught up to her.

The group walked into the first casino. Edward picked a table and began playing a game similar to blackjack, but with a deck that looked more like tarot cards. Lexy leaned towards Z who was playing next to Edward.

"Just wondering, how many times have you been to this planet?"

Just then a waitress dressed in even less clothing then Lexy eased her way between them.

"Z!," she exclaimed, throwing her arms around his neck and forcing his face into her breasts while she kissed the top of his head." I didn't think you would be back until this weekend."

Lexy leaned around the waitress, giving Z a questioning look. "She knows your name?"

The waitress tossed her hair, "Who is she?"

Lexy raised an eyebrow, leaning towards the waitress. "I'm his for the week, sweetie."

The waitress made a pouty face at Z. "But I thought I was your favorite?"

Lexy wasn't going to spend three hours with this chick. She grabbed the waitress by the arm, dragged her away from the table, and swung her around so they were face-to-face. "Let's reach an understanding here. How much will it take to make you disappear for the next three hours?"

The waitress cocked her hip out and looked Lexy up and down. "Three parts."

"Deal."

The waitress pulled a small clear device from between her breasts and Lexy placed her thumb on it and then returned to the table when the waitress walked away. The three parts was equal to sixty dollars and was well spent. She didn't want anyone to recognize Edward. Z looked disappointed.

"Lex, did you really have to get rid of her?"

"Yes, does your mother know you hang out with … that?" she asked, tugging at the hem of her skirt.

Z looked slightly panicked. "No, and it's going to stay that way."

"Now I know why you never have any extra money," she huffed and then returned her attention to the game.

Edward traveled to several different tables, gambling and ordering drinks. At one point he managed to pick up a very questionable looking woman and disappear into a back room where Apaleo and Trent stood outside the door. After half an hour he emerged and Z looked impressed.

"Did you use all your time, or did you cuddle afterwards?”

Lexy slapped the back of Z's head. “Nobody cares.” She looked at Edward, “Where to now?”

He looked at Z. “Where's the best place to get a drink and enjoy a show?”

Z rubbed his head, “I think I know a place.”

Lexy rolled her eyes and followed the group, stopping every couple of feet to pull at her skirt. Z took them to a building that looked like an everyday bar and lounge except that all the waitresses were naked and several of them we're doing inappropriate things on coffee tables in front of customers.

Edward slapped Z on the shoulder “Great choice my man,” he said, walking to the closest open table.

The look of triumph got wiped off Z's face as soon as he saw Lexy staring at him. “No more suggestions from you or I tell your mother,” she said.

Z nodded in understanding and then slipped into the chair next to Edward who was talking to a green waitress with nothing but a thong on. Lexy nodded at Trent and Apaleo to join her at the bar. From there they could watch the room to make sure no one recognized them.

Lexy ordered three drinks. “We need to at least make it look like we're here for the party, so sip slowly and don't finish it.” she instructed Trent and Apaleo.

The three of them sat and talked for what felt like

ages. Lexy looked at her watch; only thirty minutes left. She felt relief wash over her. *Just a little bit longer and then smooth sailing.*

So far Z and Edward had managed to enjoy the company of several varying beings and run up a large bar tab. Trent and Apaleo were discussing the differences between the army on Earth and the Royal Guard. *Well, I'm glad those two have found common ground.*

She took a sip of her drink and scanned the room again by way of the mirror behind the bar. Suddenly the doors opened and a group of rough looking men walked in. Lexy spit out her drink when she recognized one of them as Captain Adohan, the mercenary they'd pissed off during their last mission.

Shit!

"We have a problem," she said, reaching for a napkin to wipe her mouth and quickly mentioning who she'd seen.

Trent looked around the room while Apaleo walked slowly towards Edward; his hand reaching for the weapon under his shirt. Lexy began to stand as Captain Adohan walked up to her. Trent moved to stand next to her but someone from Adohan's group blocked him.

"Captain Lexy Greggs. What a pleasure it is to see you again," Adohan hissed.

Khunda

Lexy looked around the room, noticing more mercenaries moving towards Edward's table.

"Adohan, sorry to be rude, but we were just leaving."

Adohan put his sausage-like hand on Lexy's shoulder and forced her back onto the stool. Trent made a move toward her, causing the mercenary blocking him to put a hand on his chest and push him back into the wall.

"Adohan, we don't need to do this. We can just go our separate ways," Lexy pushed his hand off her shoulder.

From where she sat she could see the stand-off between Apaleo and two of the mercenaries. Z was currently standing on the table with his hand on his weapon saying some very unpleasant words to the three mercenaries trying to move toward Edward. Lexy couldn't see a way out of this without fighting. She knew Adohan had it out for her since their last encounter.

Fuck it.

Lexy searched to make eye contact with Apaleo, giving him a nod. She knew he understood. She brought her knee up to make contact with Adohan's groin. In a second, fighting erupted all around her. Trent's fist made contact with the jaw of the man in front of him. Z went invisible and Lexy could only guess he was attacking the men in front of him while Apaleo fought his way toward Edward, who was now standing on his chair, panicked.

Lexy kicked Adohan backward and rushed towards Edward. She dodged a body that flew in front of her and jumped towards him, aiming to land on the table, but someone grabbed her ankle and pulled her feet out from underneath her. She fell, hitting her head on the table. Pain shot through her head, and when she opened her eyes, the world had gone blurry. She tried to push herself up when someone grabbed a fist full of her hair and yanked her up, her toes barely brushing the ground. She clawed at the hand holding her up, but then thick fingers wrapped around her throat.

"You thought you could out fight us?" Adohan pulled Lexy's face close enough to his that she felt his breath on her cheek. "We were hired to deliver the Royal, but I think I'll take you with us as an added bonus for my crew. As for the rest of them, kill 'em," he snapped at his crew.

Lexy fought him, clawing at the hand around her neck, kicking furiously. She couldn't breathe and panic was setting in. Her vision began to blur around the edges as darkness closed in. She could see Trent fighting to get to her. Z reappeared next to him, bloody. Apaleo was fighting to get to Edward who was being escorted out by two very large men.

Lexy could hear Z's foul mouth and Trent calling her name. The next thing she knew she was dropped on the floor. She gasped and then sucked in, struggling to get air back in her lungs. Her vision began to clear and when she looked up, saw Trent holding a serving tray and Adohan touching the back of his head, which was covered in blood. Lexy tried to sit up.

Someone in the crowd yelled, "The Guard is coming!"

Adohan hollered, "Back to the ship!"

Lexy tried to stand, leaning against a chair for support. "The prince..."

She heard Trent's voice in her ear, "Lexy, are you okay?"

"The prince. Where is Edward?"

She looked around, seeing Apaleo chasing after the mercenaries as they rushed out the door. Z tackled one just before he could escape, and was furiously punching his face.

"Lexy, are you okay?" Trent asked again.

Lexy's hand gripped the front of his shirt. She made a fist and pulled him closer until his face was in front of hers. "I don't matter. Where is Edward?"

Trent stared at her blankly.

She pushed him away. "Go find him."

Trent hesitated, but did as he was told.

Lexy pushed off the chair and stumbled after him. She had made it to the doorway when Z's hand slid around her waist. "Come on Lex, we have to get out of here."

Chapter Eighteen

Lexy allowed Z to guide her along the walkway as her vision returned to normal. Her head was still throbbing with pain and she felt as if her thoughts were disconnected.

"We have to find him," she said.

"Trent and Apaleo are on it, Lex. I have to get you back to the ship to make sure you are okay," Z said, sounding concerned.

"Z, I'm fine. We have to find him. We can't let them take him."

Beings from the bar ran past them furiously, trying to make it back to their ships.

"Are the guards really here?" Lexy asked.

Z shook his head "No, Apaleo yelled that out; otherwise they would've taken you and killed us."

Back at the jump ship Z eased her into a seat.

"Khunda," Lexy said, "I need you to scan the planet for Trent and Apaleo's ConnectBands."

Khunda's voice made Lexy's head hurt. "I found them Captain. They are on the way to our location," she said.

"What about Edward?" Lexy asked, her pulse quickening.

"The prince is no longer on this planet, Captain."

The Khunda's calm voice infuriated Lexy.

"Damn it," she yelled, slamming her fist against the console and then instantly regretting it as pain shot up her arm.

Z had returned with the med kit and began to scan her from head to toe. He finished as Apaleo and Trent walked up the ramp, both bleeding from cuts in various places. Lexy looked at them expectantly. Trent shook his head.

"Did you guys see which way they went?" she asked.

"No Captain," Apaleo said, grabbing a couple packs of gauze out of the med kit and handing one to Trent. The two began to mop up their cuts.

"Does anyone have any ideas of how to get him back?" she snapped.

Z was sitting on the chair across from her, slowly

raising his hand into the air. "Would you like to know my idea?"

"I'll take anything right now," she huffed.

Z pulled what looked like a small blue crystal from his pocket. "Well, you see, when I picked out our clothes, I may have slipped a tracker into one of his pockets."

Lexy let out a sigh of relief. "You're a genius, Z."

Z placed the stone on the console. "Khunda, can you please locate this tracker?"

A small holographic planetary system sprung from the table behind them, there was a small red dot flashing on the hologram that seemed to be traveling away from Zuben Mu. Lexy stood stiffly, and leaned closer to the hologram. She looked around at the others.

"Okay. Now how are we going to board a mercenary ship, take on fifty or more armed crew members, rescue Edward, and then get back to our ship without anyone finding out?"

The room sat silent as they all thought about the odds they were up against.

Trent crossed his arms. "Is there any way to camouflage ourselves as mercenaries and sneak on board?"

Apaleo rubbed his chin. "I don't think that will work. At this point there are too many variables that would get us noticed."

"Wait a minute," Z leaned closer to the hologram, "Khunda, could you predict their flight course?"

"The tracker's projected course has 5364 options leading to uninhabited planets, 300 inhabited planets and 10 enlightened planets."

"That doesn't help," Lexy said, starting to panic.

"Wait a second Lex. Khunda, can you narrow down the projected courses for enlightened planets that do not have orbiting guard stations?"

"Yes, Z, there are three enlightened planets within the projected courses that do not have orbiting guard stations."

"Khunda, could you highlight those planets please?" Lexy shifted her weight; she must have hit her legs when she fell because her knee was throbbing.

The holograms zoomed out and three planets were highlighted. The group stood in silence, analyzing this new information. Lexy was the first to break the silence.

"Khunda, what are these planets used for?"

"The planet in the Lyra constellation is a small enlightened planet that was nearly destroyed during the last Great War. The planet in the Hercules Constellation is known as the junkyard, and the planet in the Bootes constellation is home to several monasteries."

Z shook his head. "I don't see why they would be heading to any of these."

Lexy shook her head, trying to think clearly. "What if they aren't heading to any of these planets?"

Apaleo looked confused. "Where else would they be heading?"

Lexy tilted her head to one side and then the other. "What if they're heading beyond that?"

Apaleo's face pinched. "Lexy I think your head needs to be looked at. We should take you back to the Khunda where you can get a proper evaluation."

"I'm not going back to the ship until we have the prince. Khunda, can you extend their projected course beyond planets that are within the Royals' rule?"

"Captain, would you like me to continue using the same search parameters?"

"Yes."

The hologram shrank and even more constellations were brought into view. "Captain, there is currently one enlightened planet outside of Royal rule that does not have an orbiting guard station."

A planet was highlighted in the Draco constellation.

Z's mouth fell open. "Shit Lex, is that what I think it is?"

Lexy used her hands to zoom in on the hologram. "Yes."

Trent looked more confused than ever. "What

planet is it? What am I missing?"

Lexy was still staring at the hologram. "That's the rebels' home planet."

Trent still looked confused. "What rebels?"

Lexy met his eyes. "The rebels are a group from the Leo constellation fighting against the Royal system."

Trent leaned against the table. "Okay, so what are they going to do? Use him as a bargaining chip?"

"No, you don't get it," Lexy said, shaking her head, "they have no respect for the lives of those living under Royal rule. They won't use Edward as a bargaining chip. They will use him as an example. The last time they got their hands on a royal they used a closed circuit signal to transmit his torture and eventual murder."

Trent dropped his head. "Don't get me wrong, I don't like that asshole, but we can't let them do that."

"I know," Lexy whispered.

Apaleo cleared his throat." Captain, I don't think we can go up against these guys by ourselves. Maybe if you just called up the director and tell her-"

"No. That would take too long. He'd be dead before we even get a response from the CTA. We're alone in this."

Trent and Z exchanged a look.

Z shrugged. "I'm in."

Trent stood straight, putting his hand on his hips.

"I'm in."

The three of them looked at Apaleo who had a look on his face. "I'm not letting you idiots go in there alone."

Lexy clapped her hands together "Okay, does anyone have any idea how we do this?"

Z zoomed out the hologram. He pointed to the highlighted planet in the Hercules system. "I've been there before. It's a great place to get parts, and the ship will pass right by it."

Lexy looked confused. "Okay… so you want to get them to stop for parts? But if their ship is working fine how are we going to do that?"

"If there was someone smart enough to hack into their ship using the tracking device, we could cause a malfunction in their systems," Z thought.

"Ali," Lexy said, "but she's in the Centaurus constellation by now."

Z walked over to the console and began pressing buttons. "Don't worry about that Lex, you and the muscle just need to worry about how to get us on the ship, find Edward and then get us back to the Kaunda without being noticed."

Lexy turned back to Apaleo and Trent. "Okay boys, you're up. Khunda, set a course for the junkyard planet and get us there as fast as you can. Trent, I need you to find every weapon we have. Apaleo, pull up the blueprints for their ship and figure out a way to get us on and back off without anyone seeing us."

The doors of the ship closed as they took off. Each of them went about their jobs. Apaleo pulled up the blueprint for a small category 1 ship. After changing into a pair of black pants and a button-up shirt, Lexy joined Apaleo. They settled on a plan that might fall apart if the smallest detail didn't go as planned, but they were desperate.

Ali came through, as always. She was able to activate the tracking device's pulse wave function that would cause the older ship to think there was a short circuit. All they had to do was hope that Edward would stay in one place so that the crew members didn't notice their ship's problem moved wherever he went.

After landing on the junkyard planet they had a half an hour to spare. Z used this time to pay off the attendant who knew him as a loyal customer. They each found a place to hide near the main landing dock.

Adohan's ship landed on time and just in front of the attendant's office. Lexy's heart pounded in her chest. She watched as Adohan and several members of his crew left the cargo bay and walked into the attendant's office. She knew they would have to come back out with the attendant to retrieve the parts. Just a few moments later the group left the store front and loaded into a rover, disappearing through the entrance. Once they were out of sight, Lexy took a deep breath and emerged from her hiding spot. A guard was standing at each of the mercenary ship's bay doors. Then, stopping far enough away so they couldn't make out her face, she whistled.

"Hey boys, I need help moving some gear boxes. Do you know anyone who could help?"

She unbuttoned the top button on her shirt.

The guard on the far side walked towards her. "I'd be willing to help you out. Maybe we could make a trade." He grinned and Lexy didn't like the tone in his voice.

The other guard shoved his shipmate out of the way, "I got this."

The guards argued as they walked closer to Lexy, who was watching the cargo bay as Trent and Z disappeared into the ship.

"You know what boys, I don't need help after all," Lexy said stepping backward.

The guards were getting too close for comfort. The guard with the creepy voice was close enough to see her face now, "Wait, you're that Captain."

The other guard squinted to get a better look at her, "Oh you bitch! Wait till Adohan sees what I caught for him. I might even get to play with you when he's done."

Lexy back tracked faster now. "Sorry boys, you're not my type."

She turned, running into the maze of parts behind the store. The guards were on her heels. Lexy turned left, right, left again then right again each time it felt like they were gaining on her. She began to make so many turns that she had no idea which way she'd come. Straining her hearing, she slowed. No one was behind her. No one was chasing her.

Crap, that can't be good.

Where was Apaleo? He was supposed to have her back. He was supposed to jump in if the guards got too close. Did one of them get to him first? She started searching for a way out. Each corner she turned led to more corners. She ran down aisle after aisle of six foot high spare parts. Panic began to worm its way into her gut. She hoped Z and Trent were already back at the jump ship with Edward.

She turned a corner and smacked into something hard and fleshy. Apaleo stood in front of her with a look on his face she'd never seen before.

"You should have listened to me, Lexy."

Before she could ask what he meant, his hand was around her neck. He dragged her all the way back to the mercenary ship. The whole crew stood just outside the bay doors. Adohan was in the front, just waiting. Waiting for Apaleo to deliver her.

Chapter Nineteen

Lexy's mind swirled, trying to understand what just happened. Why had Apaleo handed her over to the mercenaries?

The next few moments went by in a haze. The sound had been turned off in the world around her. Adohan said something to her, grabbing her hair and dragging her into the center of the cargo bay. The doors closed as he barked orders at the crew. Lexy was frozen on all fours, staring between her hands.

What's happening?

Adohan was circling her, yelling. The world around her was muffled, like she was sitting at the bottom of a pool. Her thoughts wouldn't connect, and it frustrated and scared her. Pain ripped through her side as Adohan's foot connected with her ribs. She tumbled onto her back she was able to see three figures standing over her. Adohan reached out grabbing the front of her shirt pulling her face close to his.

"Not so cocky without your little gray friend, huh?"

In an instant, Lexy saw the two men standing behind Adohan fall to the ground. Adohan dropped Lexy and looked at the fallen crew members. Both had laser burn marks on their back. Lexy crawled backwards until she hit the wall, then used all of her strength to stand. Z's voice came from across the bay.

"It's not polite to call people little, you asshole!"

Adohan raised his weapon and fired in Z's direction. Lexy looked around, the wall she was leaning on was empty, but someone had left a bag of tools just a foot away. She eased forward, grabbing the handle of a large wrench and raising it above her head, intent on bringing it down hard on Adohan. But he turned at the last second and stopped the wrench a second before it made contact. He drew his weapon, pressing the barrel against Lexy's forehead.

"Bitch."

Suddenly, just as he pulled the trigger, the gun was knocked from his hand by a streak of gray. Lexy used this opportunity to plant her fist into his throat. Adohan stumble backwards, sputtering and fighting for gasps of air. Lexy stepped forward, smashing her foot into his nose.

Blood gushed from his new wound. Lexy grabbed the wrench lying on the floor between them and stood over Adohan.

"Where is Edward, Z?"

The bay was silent. Panic shot through her, looking around for any sign of Z. Several steps away from her was Adohan's weapon, and leading into a dark corner was a trail of blood.

"Z!"

Frantically, Lexy followed the footsteps, reaching her arms out, hoping to feel him.

"Z! Where are you? Z!"

Tears began to push their way into her vision. Heavy boots stomped down the stairs. Someone had heard the noise. She wiped her eyes and whispered.

"Z, if you can hear me, stay invisible. There should be a med kit under the stairs. Please stay invisible."

Lexy returned to stand over Adohan.

The crew members circled her. "You take one step and I bash in his head."

Lexy widened her stance, ready for their attack. The crew looked from Lexy to the pool of blood around Adohan.

"Get her," Adohan garbled.

As one the crew stepped toward her Lexy brought the wrench over her head to strike, but someone ripped it out of her hands behind her. Another planted his fist into her gut, knocking the air from her lungs. She felt another fist strike her across the cheek, forcing a flash of light and blood to block her vision. She swung out of desperation. Someone grabbed her hand, rapping cold metal around it. She was knocked off balance. She brought her knee into her chest and kicked into the air connecting with someone's jaw. Someone cried out in pain.

More hands grabbed her free arm while two other sets of hands pressed her legs into the ground. She could feel cold metal being wrapped around the other arm and her ankles. She kicked; flailed with all of her strength. The last thing she remembered was someone's fist connecting with her jaw.

A warm white light surrounded her. She sat up with a jolt feeling as if she'd just had a nightmare she couldn't remember. Instead, she was surrounded by tall grass and wildflowers. Looking up, she saw a clear sky with two suns and the rings of a neighboring planet filling her view.

A deep blue dress she wore covered her legs. She stood and placed a flower crown back on her head. She could hear faint laughter in the distance, but something told her she didn't want to follow it. Instead, she turned and walked toward the hedge maze. She wandered through the maze letting her fingertips graze the walls. After a few moments she heard a man talking in the distance. Curious, she peeked around the corner to find Trent pacing in front of a fountain of the goddess Hectate, reading aloud from a small notebook. He was practicing a speech. Lexy covered her mouth, trying to stop the giggle from escaping, but it was too late. Trent turned and smiled when he recognized her. He set his notebook down on the bench and reached out his hand toward her.

"Where have you been hiding?"

Happiness exploded from her and all she could do was smile and take his hand. He pulled her towards him, wrapping her in a hug,

"You need to be preparing for the ceremony," he said, pulling back slightly so they were facing each other. He began to trace her face. "Tonight, during the full moon ceremony, you will become the priestess."

These words made Lexy's smile fade. "Which means you and I will never be."

Cold, wet shock flowed over her body. Lexy opened her eyes to find she was hanging by her wrists, dripping with water. It was a dream. It took her a minute to remember what had happened. Apaleo had betrayed her and now she was a prisoner on a mercenary ship. She looked around the dark room and was able to make out a table to the right covered in surgical looking tools. In front of her, Adohan dropped a bucket, his smile widening.

"Oh good, you're awake," Adohan said, touching the tools lying on the table. "I hoped you would be able to enjoy this part with me."

Lexy's breath quickened, her pulse raced. She pulled and tugged against her bindings.

Adohan picked up a sharp object that looked like a can opener. He grabbed the front of her shirt pulling her closer, allowing the blade to slide along her neck up to her shoulder. He pressed harder, cutting into her skin. Lexy clenched her teeth, not allowing herself to scream. Blood flowed down her arm and soaked her torn shirt.

Adohan did the same on the other side. "Go ahead my dear Captain, scream for me."

Lexy made eye contact with him. "You sick son of a-"

"Ah, remember what happened the last time you insulted my mother."

"Why don't you just kill me?" she spat at him.

"I will, but I shouldn't let your fit little body go to waste," he hissed, flicking the first button on her shirt open.

Lexy could feel bile trying to push its way up her

throat. She continued to fight against her bonds as Adohan flicked open two more buttons. Then his hand gripped her chin, jerking her head to one side. He licked her cheek and whispered in her ear.

"Keep fighting. I like it when they fight back."

Somewhere in the halls an alarm began to sound. Adohan froze, his eyes growing angry as he let go of Lexy. He backed up and adjusted himself saying, "We'll finish this later."

Lexy let out a sigh. She fought against her bindings, but could feel herself growing weak from the blood loss. Apaleo had betrayed them, Z was shot and she had no way of knowing if Trent and Edward were safe. She stared at the table of instruments.

I'm going to die here. Tears flooded her eyes. *I put everyone in this mess. This is my fault.*

The door slid open and when Lexy looked up, Marcus stood in the doorway. His eyes took in Lexy hanging in the center of the room covered in blood. He rushed in, placing his weapon on the table and reaching up to free Lexy's hands.

"If he's not already dead I'm going to kill him myself." he growled.

Her mind went blank and all she could do was stare at him as he cut through the ropes binding her. She let her arms fall around his neck. Lexy had never been so happy to see an ex before. His hands slid around her waist, hugging her back

"Here, keep your weight on me while I undo your feet," he instructed, releasing her from the hug before bending down to free her feet.

Once she was free he turned his attention to her arm. He took a knife from his pocket and cut a piece of her shirt. She hissed in pain as he tied it around her cut arm.

He wrapped one arm around her waist and picked up his gun with the other.

"Can you walk?"

"Yes. How did you know where I was?"

"That stowaway of yours sent me a message," Marcus smiled, "Maybe he's not completely useless."

"Trent is okay?"

Marcus flinched at her question.

"Yeah, he's fine. He was able to get the prince to the jump ship before Apaleo turned on you. He's another one I'm going to add to my list of people to kill," he said, helping her out of the room.

"Where is Apaleo? I get to kill him first."

"He disappeared after he gave you up."

In the distance she could hear raised voices and gunfire. Somewhere on this ship the mercenaries were giving Marcus' crew hell. Lexy, weak from blood loss, knew that with every step she was leaning more and more on Marcus. They made it to the cargo bay where members of Marcus's crew were scattered around. Three of them were huddled around a small gray body. Lexy's heart stopped.

She stumbled on the stairs, pushing past anyone who tried to help her. Dropping to her knees she threw her arms around Z's neck.

"Please don't be dead. I can't live without you."

Tears flowed; she couldn't hold back the emotion, seeing her best friend lying motionless. Someone patted her back.

"I knew you secretly wanted me," Z said.

Lexy hugged him harder. "You're an ass."

"Yeah, but you love me anyway."

Lexy sat up, wiping tears away and looking over his bandages. "Where are you shot?"

"It doesn't matter where," he said, waving his hand.

"Where?" Lexy narrowed her eyes at him as a member of the medical crew began to look at Lexy's arm.

Z rolled his eyes. "I was shot in my butt cheek."

"What?"

"Look, let's not talk about it."

"Where did these bandages come from?" Lexy pointed at the gauze around his shoulder and foot.

Z looked guilty. "You have to promise you won't get mad."

"Z!" Lexy snapped.

"I didn't stay invisible."

She shook her head. "I kind of knew you wouldn't."

Marcus squatted down next to Lexy.

"Lex, you and Z are going back to the Wonder on the Khunda's jump ship. I am going to stay here and make sure my crew gets out safely."

Lexy nodded and Marcus stood, continuing to give orders to the crew.

Z placed his hand on Lexy's knee. "Never tell him this, but I was glad to see him."

"Me too," she said, smiling.

Chapter Twenty

The jump ship returned to the Wonder which was orbiting the junkyard planet. From the moment they boarded, Lexy and Z were surrounded by crew members checking their wounds and running every scan possible. After what felt like ages they were finally allowed to clean up and change and then were escorted to a room where Edward sat in a chair staring out into space. When the door opened he turned, a look of relief on his face. Z, however, stormed forward yelling every insult he knew at him. Z stopped in front of him, winded.

"I know I'm all of those and more," Edward said. "You have all put up with me and I put you in harm's way."

Lexy crossed her arms.

"You're right, this is your fault," she said.

Edwards' eyes fell on Lexy. "I know. I was selfish and I messed up. I'm really sorry."

"You could've gotten us all killed."

"I know. I wish I could undo it," he said, his eyes on the floor.

"Someone thinks you're going to be a great king, I think you have a lot to learn," Lexy said.

Z eased into a chair.

"You can start apologizing by finding me an ice pack," Z said, groaning and shifting to take pressure off his bandaged butt.

Edward got up and walked toward the door. Lexy grabbed his arm, "Where is Trent?"

"I don't know. He went with Captain Zetha to get you guys."

Lexy met Z's eyes.

"Go find the newbie, Lex. I think Edward and I need to have some quality time."

Lexy left the room, taking the elevator to the cargo bay. She ignored all attempts to stop her, until she was back in the jump ship.

"Who's in charge here?" she asked.

The crew stared at her.

"I am a Captain and you will answer me. Who is in charge here?" she snapped.

A pretty pilot with blue skin and blond hair

stepped forward.

"I am ma'am. What can I do for you?" she asked.

"First off, don't call me ma'am. Secondly, where is Officer Trent?"

"Who-"

"The officer from my ship that went with Marcu-Captain Zetha to retrieve us. Where is he?"

The pilot placed a hand on Lexy's shoulder, making her flinch in pain.,

"I'm sure they will be back soon if you would like to wait in the-"

Lexy pushed her hand away, walked to the console and began pressing buttons.

The crew members looked at each other, shocked.

"Captain, is there something we can help you with?"

"No."

Lexy had opened a direct communication to the Wonder's jump ship left behind to bring the rest of the crew back. A pleasant male voice answered the other end.

"Jump ship, what can I do for you?"

"This is Captain Lexy Greggs, is Officer Trent around?"

"Ma'am the officers are currently searching the ship for the remaining members of the mercenary crew."

"You tell Captain Zetha that I want my officer

returned to the ship immediately."

"Ma'am, I don't-"

Lexy could hear Marcus say something to the pilot.

"Lexy, it's me," Marcus said. "Trent demanded to be part of the team searching the ship. I promise I will bring him back as soon as we are done here," he said.

"You better," Lexy said, slamming her hand on the button to cut the communications.

The crew members stared at her.

"I'll wait here," Lexy explained, sitting in the pilot's chair and crossing her arms.

It was an hour before the jump ship returned to the Wonder. Lexy waited impatiently. When she heard the bay door open she walked to the end of the ramp with her arms crossed.

The Wonder's jump ship eased to land in the bay. The ramp opened and several members of the mercenary crew, including Adohan, were escorted off by security officers. Trent limped down the ramp behind them, barely making it to the bottom before Lexy stormed forward to stand in front of him.

"You shouldn't have gone. You could've been killed! What happened to your leg?"

Lexy stepped back, allowing him to limp down the rest of the ramp.

"I wasn't going to let those bastards hurt you. I was also hoping that Apaleo was on that ship. When you guys didn't meet me back at the ship I came looking for you. I saw him hand you off to them. I wasn't going to be able to fight my way onto their ship myself so I made a call."

Marcus walked down the ramp, slapping Trent on the back, causing Trent to flinch.

"Yeah, lucky for him my cargo is the gambling kind," Marcus said, a cocky smirk spreading across his face.

A member of the crew took Trent by the arm, telling him they needed to take a look at his injuries. Lexy watched him limp away, thankful that her crew was safe. She noticed Marcus watching her.

"How are you feeling? You lost a lot of blood, Lex."

He sounded concerned.

"I'm fine. Your crew gave me some supplement shots."

Lexy pulled her sleeves over her hands.

"We need to get back to our ship, but first I want to make sure this doesn't get back to the CTA or the Royals," she said, staring at her hands. "I'm fine conceding to you being the better Captain, but if this gets out the CTA will be in jeopardy. And because of Apaleo's actions there could be some backlash on the humanoid races."

Marcus took her by the hands to stop her fidgeting.

"Lexy, you have to know that I would never do anything to harm you or any other humanoid. And as far as my cargo and crew are concerned, we were simply orbiting Zuben Mu since our cargo spent the night on the planet."

Lexy smiled, but couldn't help thinking there was a catch.

"What do you want?" she asked.

A guilty smile spread across his face.

"What do you mean?"

Lexy let him slide his finger between hers.

"I know you Marcus. What do you want for keeping your mouth shut?"

Marcus laughed, "Never the one for being coy, were you Lexy?"

She raised her eyebrow.

"How about dinner and a long talk about what went wrong with us?"

"Of course." Lexy pulled her fingers from his and walked toward the elevators.

Marcus stood there, unsure of her reaction. "So, was that a yes?"

"Fine," she sighed as the elevator doors closed.

Chapter Twenty-One

After returning to the Khunda, Lexy found the crew much more subdued. Edward stayed in his quarters like he promised. Lexy hoped that Z's chat with him had matured him a little. She, Z and Trent hid on the bridge, staring into the black. It wasn't until they were about to land on Alpha Virgo that anyone said a word.

They landed to a King's welcome. People lined the streets as well as the rooftops, cheering so loudly their ears rang for several hours afterwards. There was no indication that anyone knew what had happened. The crew was met by religious leaders from the planet who prayed over them, wiped oil on their foreheads and handed them small cakes. Lexy did her best to smile, but the events of the night before began to weigh on her. She started to feel panicky and exhausted at the same time. Once the welcoming was over she asked to go to her room. A beautiful young elf breed led the way. Lexy stared at the back of the girl's head.

She thought she could be Ali's sister. Elf breed genetics didn't vary much.

Once in her room Lexy buried herself in the blankets, shoes and all. Hiding from the universe, she fell into a borage of nightmares, but was jolted awake by the elf girl's soft voice.

"Captain, are you okay?"

Lexy shifted and moaned.

"Captain, I have to get you ready for the ceremony."

Lexy threw the covers off and found three elf girls at the end of the bed, staring. The girls helped her into the bath. Lexy took a handful of salts and began scrubbing every inch of her skin, hoping to scrub away the memories, as well. After the bath her hair was braided and she was helped into another formal dress.

Z and Trent arrived at her door. Both were stone-faced, like her. Z broke the silence.

"You okay, Lex?"

"I'm fine," she said, leading the way out of the room.

The ceremony was as expected, stuffy and too long for their liking. The three of them spoke only when spoken to, not caring what anyone else thought. Lexy felt like she was walking through a haze the entire evening. Beautiful beings and stunning gowns passed her, but it was as if she didn't even see them. Thankfully, during the royal dinner the three of them were placed at the far end of the table. Lexy stared blankly ahead and watched Edward smile and chat happily with his new Council. She couldn't be angry at him. This is what he was raised for. This was his sole purpose in life. He was simply happy to be alive in order to live it.

Lexy, on the other hand, knew what was waiting for her back at the CTA. She would have to explain why Apaleo was no longer with them. The thought of coming clean to Ameran made her throat tighten. Lexy looked for the closest door, set down the glass that had somehow appeared in her hand, and slid outside. She walked down the stairs and along the path until she was standing on top of a hill. Placing her hand on her stomach, she took in several shaky breaths, and without even realizing it, tears began to flow down her face.

Trent walked up behind her and placed his hand on her lower back, leading her behind a hedge. The space was dark, but she knew he was standing just behind her, allowing her tears to flow. When her sobs began to slow, Trent handed her a piece of cloth to dry her eyes. Lexy slowly regained her composure and the two returned to the party. Z kept his eyes on Lexy without saying a word.

The next morning the crew prepared the ship for takeoff. Lexy was overseeing the unloading of Edwards belongings when he walked up the ramp.

"I didn't know you would leave so soon."

Lexy brushed her hair from her eyes.

"I need to get back to the CTA. The director needs to know about Apaleo."

The newly crowned king rolled back on his heels.

"I wanted to thank you again for saving my life. I know I didn't make any of this easy."

Lexy shook her head. "Apaleo had already planned to betray us. I see that now. That explains why he chose such a young crew. They were less likely to stand in his way and it could've been worse if we were aboard the Khunda. People would have gotten hurt or killed"

"Either way," Edward stared at a small box wrapped in blue paper he was holding, "I am indebted to you. If there is anything you need-"

Lexy placed her hand on his.

"I won't come to you," she smiled at him. "Z, on the other hand may stop by for guys' night every once a while."

Edward laughed.

"He is welcome anytime, and so are you."

He looked at the box again.

"Here," he handed it to Lexy, "I found this in the library. It belonged to a very strong woman who lived here years ago. She was said to be of the ancient Virgo bloodline.

I read about her in the academy. She reminds me of you."

Lexy tore the paper off revealing a small diary. She flipped through the pages in awe of the delicate handwriting.

"I can't accept this-" she said, trying to push the diary back into his hands

But Edward stepped backward.

"It belongs to you, my Captain."

Lexy smiled as Edward turned and walked down the ramp.

Trent walked up behind her.

"What did he want?"

Turning to face him she smiled.

"To thank us."

Trent snorted. "Ass."

The trip back to the CTA was uneventful. Lexy took to hiding in her quarters. She found herself panicking when she was around large groups of people.

"Captain, you received a video message." Khunda said.

"Patch it through, Khunda."

Lexy slid off the couch, tidying her hair the best she could.

The screen next to her door flashed, filling with the Dali Lama's face. Lexy almost burst into tears.

"Hello, Captain." the old man's face was wrinkled but his friendly smile reminded Lexy of a young child. "I hope my message finds you well. I heard on the news that Alpha Virgo got a new King. I hope your journey was a smooth one. I am in the Gemini constellation helping with the refugees from the recent meteor strike. I would love to meet soon. I have a new tea I believe you would enjoy. Send me any time you have availability and I will do my best to find a way to meet with you. Namaste, Captain."

The message ended with his soft laugh. Lexy wiped away her tears before sending him a response. She explained that the transport didn't go as planned but everything managed to work out. She promised to sen him a message the next time she was out for a mission. After hitting send Lexy found herself with a little more courage than she had before. Taking a deep breath she returned to the bridge, giving Z and Trent a smile before taking her seat. The tension between the three of them seemed to fade away. Trent and Lexy spent an hour trading butt jokes at Z's expense. He happily accepted the banter, seeing that it made Lexy laugh.

When they landed at the CTA docks four members of the guard met them.

"This can't be good," Z said, crossing his arms. The rest of the crew stared after them as they walked up the dock.

Lexy, Z and Trent were escorted to Ameran's office.

All three of them sat quietly while she paced behind her desk.

"Can one of you tell me why I am missing my top security officer?"

Lexy stood. "Director, can I speak with you in private?"

Trent and Z both began to argue at her request.

Ameran held her hand up.

"The Captain's request stands. You two, outside."

Trent and Z walked out onto the landing, leaned against the wall and watched as Lexy talked and at times Ameran yelled. After several minutes, Ameran hugged Lexy.

"Girls are weird," Z said, watching the exchange.

Lexy walked out to meet Z and Trent at the door.

Ameran swung her door open, allowing Lexy to walk through first.

"You three are the luckiest sons of bitches I have ever met."

Z was shocked.

"Does this mean we're not fired?"

She crossed her arms.

"You are on probation. You three get non-living cargo from now until I say different."

Trent raised his hand.

"Ma'am, did you just say 'you three?'"

The Director opened her office door to walk back through.

"Yes, Trent, you are the new head of security for the Khunda. Don't make me regret it."

Ameran turned on her heels and returned to her office.

Z laughed.

"Well, it looks like you're stuck with us newbie."

Lexy led the way into the tube.

"Come on, Z. You can drop us back off on Earth. My Uncle is probably having a fit trying to cover up your absence." She said, looking at Trent in his CTA security gear. "And I could really go for some chocolate pie."

Trent leaned against the railing next to her, crossing his arms.

"Not to mention you owe me dinner."

Z slowly turned, his mouth hanging open.

"You agreed to have dinner with him?"

Lexy dropped her head, pushing the palm of her hands into her eyes.

This is going to be a long trip home.

Thank you for reading. Please leave an honest review on Amazon.

If you would like to get notified when upcoming titles are being released you can follow my Amazon author page or sign up for my newsletter on my website (www.KristinaBakBooks.com) for extra information about this book and more.

Khunda

272

Rebellion

(Ancient Blood Book 2)

Chapter One Sneak Peek

Khunda

Chapter One

Lexy Greggs stared at the three silver stars of insignia as they reflected the light pouring into Ameran's office, the head of the Capital Transport Agency or CTA. A soft layer of dust coated the glass that protected the insignia. Three stars was the top rank a Captain could get. Lexy pulled her sleeve over her hand and wiped the dust away. Her mother's image smiled at her, causing Lexy's heart to ache. She was sixteen when her parents died in an attack on their ship, and ever since the funeral, her mother's stars hung on the wall behind Ameran's desk.

Lexy began to pace in front of the wall-to-ceiling windows.

"Lex, stop. You're worrying over nothing," Zephla, or Z as everyone called him, said his feet propped up on the desk. Ameran hated when he did that. Z was a gray alien and they had a special skill for pissing people off.

"It's not like we've ever gotten good news when she calls us to her office, Lexy said, "I keep running through our missions for the past month. I can't think of anything we messed up." She stopped pacing and glared at Z. They had been best friends their whole life, and he was the biggest troublemaker she knew. "Is there anything I should know about? Did you fuck something up?"

Trent, the head of security, sat in the chair next to Z and chuckled.

Z looked from Lexy to Trent in fake shock, "How dare you accuse me of doing something to damage our chances of getting normal missions again. Do you think I enjoyed cleaning out the cargo bay after that last shipment of pigs from Beta Leo? Honestly."

Lexy shook her head and began pacing again.

Trent shifted to lean his elbows on his thighs, "Lexy, I don't think she called us here for bad news."

Z beamed at Lexy.

"However," Trent continued, "is there anything you need to tell us, Z?"

"Oh, come on. Do you really not trust me?"

"No," both Lexy and Trent responded.

"Whatever," Z scuffed.

Z's small gray form slumped in the chair. He began mumbling under his breath. Lexy rolled her eyes and paced. She had been walking on eggshells for the past month, and her gut twisted every time she thought about the stress she brought on Ameran. The woman was her mother's best friend and looked after Lexy as much as possible without it looking like favoritism. She hated that Ameran and the CTA were now under close watch by the Council and the Royal families.

All because a spoiled King got himself kidnapped on her mission.

A long stream of air escaped her lips as she glanced at the case holding her mother's life's work. She couldn't let her parents down. She had to prove that she was worth a third star.

Woosh.

Lexy spun on her heel, barely keeping her balance, but restarted her pacing when a short brown and gray reptilian breed brought in a tray of tea and water.

"Director Ameran is on her way. Would you like any refreshment while you wait?" he asked.

Lexy shook her head before stopping to look out the window at the CTA docks below.

Z jumped out of the chair and walked over to the tray. "Do you have anything a little stronger?"

The reptilian sneered, "No."

Z sighed. "I keep telling Ameran she needs to get some better options. Not all of us can be stuffy saints like this guy." He jabbed his thumb at the reptilian, who hissed in response.

Trent stood. "I'm sorry about our pilot's comments. He is just a bit tired and antsy. Would you happen to know if we will have to wait much longer?"

The reptilian's mouth twitched upwards into a shy smile. "Yes, it should be just moments."

"Could I get a cup of tea?" Trent flashed his pearly whites, and Lexy snorted under her breath. The reptilian went straight to work pouring and asking how he took his tea. Once he was finished, the reptilian left the tray and hurried out of the room.

Trent's ability to charm any being he came across still amazed her. He was new to the concept of alien life. A month ago, he was just another ignorant Earthling going about his business until he dove aboard the *Khunda*'s jump ship to save Lexy from danger. Little did he know it was her ship. In just a few hours, his world went from one form of intelligent life to thousands.

He was adapting well to his new position aboard *Khunda*. He even spent a few days at Area 51 without Earth's Extraterrestrial Response Unit, also known as the Men in Black, getting any information out of him.

They're dumbasses.

The door slid open again, and Ameran, a tall thin woman with blue skin, walked in, followed by a dark-skinned man with gills.

He must be one of the hybrid species the grays created before the war.

Lexy stepped forward, "Director, it's a pleasure to see you again."

The formality felt odd to her, but she knew it was needed if the man accompanying her was there to keep an eye on things.

Ameran nodded coldly, causing Lexy's stomach to twist.

"Captain Lexy Greggs, this is Claes of Polemis, a new member of the Council."

Shit.

Lexy's face must have dropped because Claes waved his hand, "I am not that kind of Council member. I am in training, if you will."

Ameran stepped behind her desk as Lexy shook Claes' smooth hand. The texture reminded her of petting a dolphin.

"Polemis. Isn't that one of the Gray planets? I didn't realize you had representation on the Council." Lexy asked.

Trent pushed another chair to Ameran's desk and motioned for Claes to take it. Lexy stood next to the chair Z had already taken, and he was examining an artifact taken from a nearby shelf.

"Yes," Claes answered, sitting, "I was allowed to sit in on Council meetings for the last four years as a trial run. This is my first year as an official member."

Lexy nodded in understanding. Many of the enlightened species didn't view the Gray planets with respect. So, Lexy was happy to hear they were allowed some representation on the Council.

"Captain Greggs," Claes went on, "when I was alerted to this case, I read up on your history, and first, I would like to express my thanks for your parents and their devotion to the CTA and protecting their cargo. Because of them, a great scientist is alive."

Z huffed, and Lexy glared at him before responding.

"Thank you for that. I assure you that I take my parent's sacrifice seriously."

Ameran nodded, "I explained this to Council member Claes, but he is here for a more important reason. The council has called the crew of *Khunda* for questioning about the events of the Alpha Virgo royal mission."

Z dropped the artifact in his lap, "I thought we were moving on from that?" he asked, his voice an octave higher than usual.

Lexy took the artifact from his hand and placed it on Ameran's desk, "I'm sorry, but I'm not sure why we are being called in for questioning. We filed our reports in accordance with the Royal Guard's guidelines, and Edward-," Lexy took a breath, "I mean, King Edward praised the CTA for our rescue of him from Adohan's ship in his coronation speech. We did everything we could to complete the mission. I'm not sure what other questions they could have. What are they looking for?"

Claes glanced at Ameran before responding.

"Some members of the Council have been pushing for a vote on the gray planets."

"Why? The Gray planets have been in the courts for centuries, so, why would they want to push through a vote now?" Lexy crossed her arms, "And the newsfeeds haven't said anything about it. Wouldn't this be front-page news?"

"The members have wanted to keep it quiet until they know if it will happen. They are worried that the news of a vote could cause an increase in attacks by the rebels." Claes responded, not making eye contact with her.

"Do you have any idea which way the vote could go?" Trent asked.

Ameran took a deep breath.

"That bad, huh?" Z huffed.

"Unfortunately, over the last few years, members of the two enlightened gray planets have joined with the rebellion. Three Royals were assassinated in the last year. And in some of the council member's eyes, your Royal mission was just another sign that the Gray planets were a mistake."

"That wasn't us. We were betrayed." Lexy spat.

Ameran cleared her throat, "We know that, but Apaleo was from a Gray planet."

Silence fell over them.

Trent rested his elbows on his knees. "They feel threatened by the rebellion." His voice sounded strained, as if he just realized Earth's future was on the chopping block because of the choices made by beings light-years away. "They can't wipe out three planets because of the actions of a few," Trent said, more to himself than to the group.

Claes shifted to look at Trent, "They can and they will. The rebellion's numbers are growing, and some members of the Council feel that the Royal system is being threatened." He turned back to face Lexy, "you must not have heard."

Her gut twisted at the tone in his voice.

"A Royal was captured, tortured, and killed on a live feed two days ago."

Lexy dropped to sit on the arm of Z's chair, her hand over her mouth.

Z's voice sounded far off as Lexy's mind raced, "Couldn't they stop the damn feed?"

Claes sighed, "No, the encryption was impenetrable. They must have some new techs on their side."

Ameran was staring out of the window, "The worst part is that they mentioned Apaleo."

"Fuck," Z threw up his hands, "I knew that dick would come back to bite us in the ass."

Ameran's eyes narrowed at Z, "Don't let Zephla talk at your questioning."

"Hey...no, never mind. That's probably a good idea." Z settled back in the chair.

Lexy glanced at her mother's stars, her jaw clenched. Unable to calm her frustration, she looked at Trent, who rubbed the stubble that Z had told him would get him chicks. His eyes connected with hers. She knew he was just as worried. His arms flexed as he rubbed his hands together. His eyebrow raised, letting her know he was with her. Lexy already knew Z was ride-or-die, but she looked at him to see his reaction. He was staring at his shoes. She knew Z was still upset that he didn't see Apaleo's betrayal coming, and felt guilty. The same guilt she felt even though she knew it wasn't her fault. Lexy placed her hand on his shoulder. He looked up at her and shrugged.

Lexy took a deep breath and stood, adjusting her CTA jacket. "I assume Council member Claes is here to inform us of the questioning, officially, " Claes nodded, "And I also assume we cannot reject the Council's request."

He shook his head.

Ameran cleared her throat, "You wouldn't want to try, either."

"Why the fuck not?" Z mumbled.

Claes chuckled. Ameran shifted on her chair.

"Because they will freeze all of your assets. Khunda included. You would not be allowed to work for any company while you stand your ground in protest, and oh yeah, they will put you in jail." Ameran laced her thin blue fingers, resting them on her lip, and narrowed her eyes at Z.

He rolled his eyes, "Oh, that's all."

Lexy looked from Claes to Ameran. It was the first time she noticed a small section of Ameran's black hair had escaped her tight bun. Lexy scanned her face picking up on small details she had overlooked. Her eyes were red around the edges, and the crease between her eyebrows looked a little deeper.

Lexy realized that she was dealing with more than she was letting on. Shifting her focus back to Claes, Lexy lifted her chin higher.

"When is the questioning?"

Claes stood, his face unreadable.

Shit, this can't be good.

"Captain Greggs of the class A transport ship, Khunda, you are being summoned to the Council chambers for questioning. Do you have anything to say?"

Lexy extended her wrists toward him, "No."

Claes wrapped a thin silver band around each wrist. The metal was cool and light. It was designed to subdue and track a prisoner without bringing any unwanted attention. Trent jumped out of his chair, his hand reaching out to stop Claes. His face reminded her of a lion protecting the pride. Ameran's light touch made him pause. She shook her head, letting her hand slide off his shoulder.

"Wait, we're doing this shit now?" Z questioned.

Ameran rubbed her temples, "I thought you weren't going to talk until after the questioning?"

"Do you know me?" Z's large eyes looked at each of them, "No, really, does she know who she is talking to?"

Lexy rolled her eyes, "He will do his best, ma'am."

Z stood next to Lexy, his gray arms extended, "I assume that means the whole crew is invited?"

Claes nodded and wrapped a pair of bands on Z's wrists. Then, he turned to Trent, "As head of security, do you have any objections?"

With one last glance at Ameran, Trent held out his wrists, "No, sir."

Lexy rubbed the lightweight bracelets, smiling at Trent. His lips pulled into a tight smile. Her gut tightened, making her wish she hadn't eaten so much at lunch. Being questioned by the council wasn't what she had hoped the meeting would be about, but life has ways of kicking you in the ass.

Claes turned to Ameran, "I will bring them back as soon as the questioning is over."

"Thank you, Claes. I hope they cooperate and keep the profanity to a minimum." She looked at Z, who shrugged.

"I make no promises."

Lexy loved his smart-ass comments, but she hoped he would control himself for once in his life. Claes motioned for Lexy to go first. She took one last glance at Ameran, who was leaning against her desk with her arms crossed. Her face resembled Aunt May's when Lexy left for her service in the Royal Guard. She must be worried about the outcome.

They walked in silence. Beings walked past them, glancing at the silver bands. Lexy pulled her sleeves down. As they walked through the CTA's doors, two beings, a plant crossbreeds by the look of them, began whispering to each other. News of the questioning must have spread further than Ameran's office. Maybe there was a mole in the Council's chambers. They walked down to the docks, the sun shining. It was a typically perfect day on Alpha Orion. There were only two seasons here, and they were at the end of the longest spring-like season.

Lexy scanned the city skyline. Tall silver buildings scattered the main island like crystals growing in a cave. Small crafts weaved through the buildings, reflecting the few clouds that dotted the sky. Even across the water, Lexy could see the blue haze of the fountains that circled the city. Each of them connected to underground aquatic tunnels for gilled species to use.

Claes stopped at the end of the dock next to a small shuttle, and he held out his hand to help Lexy in. She gave him a small smile and let him help her. She eased herself into the seat next to the steering controls. As the others climbed aboard, she looked over her shoulder at Khunda, one dock over. The large ship hovered silently above the water. She wiped away a tear as Claes started the engine, and

they headed toward the Council building in the center of the main island.

The Rebellion Begins!

Available Now!

Khunda

About the Author

Kristina Bak is a Georgia based author of science fiction and fantasy novels.
While in college, Kristina began to write her first novel, Khunda. In 2016, she attempted her first NaNoWriMo. In 2017, she completed Khunda with the love and support of her NaNoWriMo family.
In her spare time she enjoys ice dancing, yes Georgia has ice rinks. Kristina lives with her husband, son and two fur babies, Bones and Zoe.

Khunda